The Yellow Tiger

By G. H. Teed

From *The Sexton Blake Library*,
1st Series, No. 1, September 1915.

Stillwoods Edition, 2019

Stillwoods.Blogspot.Ca

Catalogue Information:
Title: The Yellow Tiger.
Author: G. H. Teed (1886-1938)
First published in: *The Sexton Blake Library*, 1st Series, No. 1,
September 1915.
This Edition by: Stillwoods, 2019. (Doug Frizzle)
ISBN Canada: 978-1-988304-88-5
Blog: Stillwoods.Blogspot.Ca
Author Blog: http://ghteed.blogspot.com/
Storefront: http://www.lulu.com/spotlight/lulubook22

Keywords: Sexton Blake, British fictional detective, Wu Ling

Trivia:
There is a section on Westward Ho! And its golf course. Included in the evidence of a crime are a description of the various golf clubs which were used in 1915. The golf club still exists and has a website.

While I was digitizing "The Great Air Mystery", a Nelson Lee Library story, the cover image promoted the story saying it was done by the author of "The Yellow Tiger" but I knew no such Nelson Lee story existed so I looked around for such a Teed story and located this work. It shows how Amalgamated Press was intertwined with Sexton Blake and Nelson Lee stories—there was a time when both names were copyrighted and owned by Amalgamated.

This was the first issue of the Sexton Blake Library magazine which lasted from 1915 to 1968.

Synopsis:
Featuring both criminal organizations, the German, Council of Eleven, and the Chinese, Brotherhood of the Yellow Beetle this is a fast action kidnapping of the British Munitions Minister. But while Sexton Blake breaks this case, he is himself kidnapped. As the foremost problem for Prince Wu Ling, his death will be a tribute in China. Blake is in transit to Kaitu Island but the British nation with Yvonne and Tinker will do anything to save Blake—to their peril.

Fast action, this is a classic, long Sexton Blake story which presages problems with Germany and China.

Under the Eagle's Wing
The Rogues' Republic
The Mitcham Murder Mystery
The Brotherhood of the Yellow Beetle

See http://ghteed.blogspot.com/
For some of G. H. Teed's shorter works.

The island of Marsey, which lies just off the Welsh coast beneath the frowning cliff of Pembroke, is as lonely a spot as one will find in all the kingdom. It forms a rough triangle in the sea, the legs of which are each about two miles in length. One small bay alone permits a landing, and with that exception the shores are high, rugged cliffs, the haunt of the sea-bird and the home of Neptune's thunder.

The island itself is almost devoid of habitants or habitations. One large bungalow, built by a former owner, gives on to the small cove where a landing-stage has been built; and a second, the only other building, is an ancient farmhouse, fashioned centuries ago from rudely-hewn timbers, and at present the home of the farmer-fisherman, tenant of the present owner of the island.

For the rest, the island is the grazing-ground of sheep and cattle belonging to the owner, and which are looked after on a share basis by the farmer. Beyond that the rabbits hold sway, falling by thousands each year into the traps of the farmer.

A narrow sound of less than two miles in width separates the island from the mainland, yet, narrow as is that sound, it was, in days gone by, the scene of many stirring scenes when smuggler and excise man met and clashed together.

No lighthouse is there to send forth its beacon each night to the ships which pass up and down the wide highway beyond, and for that reason it is a place shunned by the mariner and fisherman alike. For years it formed part of a large estate on the mainland and was seldom favoured by the visits of the landlord.

But lately when that estate was broken up it was bought in by a man who was a stranger to the district, and who, though well-known in certain quarters, was unknown in name or fame to the local inhabitants.

The purchaser was Baron Robert de Beauremon, president of that daring criminal organisation known as the Council of Eleven. Why he had bought it, or to what purpose he intended to put it, none knew.

The farmer tenant was informed by Beauremon's solicitors that the stock on the island had been bought by Beauremon, and that the arrangement which he had with the former owner would continue as usual. To the farmer-fisherman this was satisfactory, and he continued his duties as usual, scarcely troubling himself with thoughts of the new owner.

But a mild feeling of excitement filled him when he received a letter informing him that Baron Robert de Beauremon was coming to the island with some friends, and requesting him to get the bungalow in order. The tenant proceeded to do so, remarking to himself that the owner had neglected to say how he would arrive or by what means he would get across to the island.

Three days later he was enlightened with something of a shock, when, as he stood on the landing-stage in the little cove, he saw what at first appeared to be some strange colossal bird high overhead and winging its way towards the island.

As it approached, it grew larger and larger until, to the startled gaze of the tenant it resolved itself into one of the great air machines of which he had read and seen in pictures, but which he had never witnessed in reality.

Nor was his astonishment any the less when it swooped down towards the island and came to earth on a wide stretch of level field where cattle grazed. The beasts with tails in the air tore off madly towards a distant wood, and the farmer, running towards the spot where the huge biplane had come down, met two men climbing out of the cockpit.

One of them, a tall, fair man of commanding presence, removed his flying helmet as the tenant came up, and, smiling genially, informed him that he was the baron. The other man he indicated as Senor Gonzalez, his friend, following up the statement by asking if the bungalow had been got ready. The tenant, scarcely able to reply from the amazement which filled him, stammered out an affirmative and led the way towards it.

Then he was kept on the move as he had never been before. The new owner wanted this and that attended to, and nothing would do but he must make a complete tour of the island that very day.

For two days he was here, there, and everywhere, and then on the third night there was a new arrival. The farmer-tenant knew not whence he came. His first knowledge of the arrival was when the baron and his friend arranged a strong light on the landing-stage in the cove, and by its beams lighted in a large motor-boat which arrived late at night.

The tenant received a further shock when he saw that the new arrival was a Celestial, and that the one man who formed the crew of the motor-boat was also a Chinaman.

Then the two new arrivals disappeared towards the bungalow with their host, and the tenant saw no more of them for twenty-four hours.

But had he been able to conceal himself beneath the wide balcony of the bungalow he would have heard something which would have given him cause to think.

That same night, when the new arrivals had been refreshed by a plain but plentiful meal, Baron Robert de Beauremon and one of the Celestials went out on to the balcony, and seating themselves in low wicker chairs bent towards each other.

It was the baron who spoke first.

"How do things progress, prince?" he asked in a low tone, though in truth they had only the sea-birds for eavesdroppers.

Prince Wu Ling—for it was he—shrugged slightly.

"My arrangements are complete," he replied. "It is only for you to say the word."

Beauremon was silent for a little, then he said:

"When you first made the proposal to me, prince, I was dubious of its possibilities, but as I told you then I was and am prepared to go ahead with it, providing there was sufficient in it to tempt me. Of course, you know about the Council of Eleven, and will understand that we can only take on propositions which promise a large reward. It takes a lot of money to run such an organisation as the Council of Eleven, and we have been a little unfortunate lately.

"However, I am down here to listen to a definite offer, and if I take it up I am ready to act at once. If not —well, you will be a welcome guest as long as you will honour me with your presence."

"You speak fairly, baron," responded Wu Ling. "I understand the difficulties which are yours, and I understood them before I approached you regarding this affair. But I think the financial reward will be sufficient for you.

"Some time ago—it matters not exactly when—I was in communication with certain sources to whom Britain's power and present policy are inimical. At that time I joined forces with these people, and it was my intention to carry out for them certain operations in return for which they offered me their assistance in affairs which are very near my heart.

"I shall not bore you by a relation of the first step in this

3

agreement. Sufficient is it to say that owing to laxity on the part of someone it was a failure, due principally to the meddling of a man whom you have reason to hate as much as I."

"You mean—" said Beauremon.

"I mean Sexton Blake," replied Wu Ling curtly. "Time and again has that man intruded himself upon my affairs, but one day—one day—ah! my friend! one day he will fall into my power. Then—" And Wu Ling finished with an expressive shrug. "But that is beside the question," continued the prince. "As I said, the first affair was muddled. It is my intention that there shall be no muddling in the second. For that reason I have laid my plans carefully, and have sought you, baron. Together we can do much."

"If we are successful it will take not more than a week of your time. If we are unsuccessful—but I will not consider that possibility. I am determined that we shall be. For the reward I can promise you a substantial sum for our co-operation. I am prepared to offer you ten thousand pounds down and, if success is ours, add to that another ten thousand."

"That would make twenty thousand in all," murmured the baron. "Make it twenty-five thousand in the event of success, prince, and my answer is 'Yes'."

Wu Ling shrugged.

"As you will," he replied. "It shall be twenty-five thousand. And now to the details. My present allies are, as I have already told you, interested in certain affairs here in England. They have planned a series of coups, all of which lead up to a main coup, the nature of which even I do not know.

"I speak of the Germans. To them I have promised my aid, in return for which they give me theirs, as I have told you. Now I understand, baron, that it is an essential part of the conditions governing the Council of Eleven that there shall be no question of creed or country to influence your operations. Am I right?"

Beauremon nodded.

"That is quite right, Prince Wu Ling. The Council of Eleven is prepared to work for anyone, providing, the price is paid."

Wu Ling smoked in silence for a few moments, then continued:

"Do you know the new British Minister of Munitions, baron?"

"I do not know him personally," replied Beauremon. "But I have seen him often."

4

Wu Ling held up one thin, yellow hand.

"Baron, that man is one of the geniuses of the age. He is probably one of the best-hated and best-loved men who ever lived. When he is spoken of there is no lukewarm sentiment expressed. It is either profound admiration or violent dislike. Yet no man has been watched more closely by the enemies of Britain than he. And it is true that these British pigs owe a vast deal to his brains.

"He has been the strong man at the helm—it is his keen mind which has seen through the muddles created by others, and now when the British have at last awakened, and have begun to realise that only strenuous measures will meet the tremendous demands upon them, they have had the sense to turn to this one man to lead them through the maze.

"With his usual promptitude he has risen to the demands made upon him, and when I say that he is the greatest enemy Germany has, I only speak the truth. Therefore, you will not be surprised to know that Germany is determined to remove him from the scene.

"Without him some muddler will take charge of things, and that will be another step ahead in the German programme which aims to lull this country into a state of security until the Germans are ready for the grand effort. Do you follow me?"

"Perfectly," responded Beauremon. "Proceed, please."

"It is to seek your assistance in removing this man from the scene of affairs that I have sought your aid," went on Wu Ling. "This island is, as it happens, ideally situated for the purpose. Your organisation will complete the circle of conditions necessary to make the situation perfect. Now I have learnt that this Munitions Minister is to leave London tomorrow night by motor-car for North Devon.

"He will visit at Northam, which is near the Westward Ho! golf-links, and on Saturday and Sunday will play golf. Golf is his only relaxation at present, and the only means he has of keeping fit while working at the pressure he is. I have a plan of the golf-links, and will show it to you.

"In a word, my plan is to get possession of the person of the Munitions Minister while he is playing golf at Westward Ho! With your assistance, and the use of your passenger-carrying aeroplane, I am strongly convinced that the thing can be carried out successfully. That is the proposition, baron. Are you prepared to take it up?"

Beauremon did not reply at once, but smoked thoughtfully for some minutes. Finally he roused himself.

"It is a highly dangerous proposal you outline," he said slowly. "If it can be brought off it will be one of the biggest coups on record—to kidnap a British Cabinet Minister! Nor would that be the end of it. The moment his absence was discovered, the best brains in the country would be at work to discover his whereabouts, and it would have to be a lonely place indeed which would suffice to hide him."

"But he wouldn't be kept hidden long," murmured Wu Ling softly. "A few days only would suffice, then he would never more be seen in this life."

"So that is the game, is it?" muttered the baron. "Frankly, prince, I don't like it. But I said I was prepared to enter into any arrangement you proposed, providing the price was sufficient, and I will not draw back. But we shall have to tread very warily indeed. This particular Cabinet Minister is no fool, I assure you."

"He is a dog, and will meet the fate of a dog!" rejoined Wu Ling passionlessly. "And since that is agreed upon, baron, suppose we call the others and discuss the details with them?"

Beauremon rose, and going to the door which led into the living-room of the bungalow, spoke in a low tone to the two men who sat there. One, a stout, powerful-looking Chinaman, rose at once, and bowed politely, waiting until the other man should rise too.

Had it been possible for Sexton Blake, the great London criminologist, to have peeped into that room just then, he would have recognised the Celestial as San, the shrewd and faithful lieutenant of Prince Wu Ling. And it was by this name Beauremon also knew him.

The other man, a small, swarthy-looking individual, whose every movement was as lithe as those of a panther, was Gonzalez, the Spanish member of the Council of Eleven, and the aviator of that organisation. He it was who had driven the great passenger-carrying biplane which had brought Beauremon to the island a few days before.

Both he and San followed the baron out on to the balcony and joined in the discussion. Until far into the night they talked, and when they finally rose to retire, all the details had been settled.

So as they sought their rooms with the distant pounding of the waves, the only sound to break the quietude of the lonely island, they had completed their plans. And at daybreak they began to put them into operation. Beauremon was abroad just as morn mounted out of the East.

The other three appeared on the balcony soon after, and when a hasty breakfast had been consumed, they all made their way to the shed where the biplane had been left. Gonzalez and Beauremon wheeled it out, and for some minutes the Spaniard was busy tuning up. Then he signed to the baron that the machine was ready, and the baron turned to Wu Ling.

"It is ready, prince. Shall we get along?"

Wu Ling nodded, and Beauremon led the way into the hangar. There he and Wu Ling donned flying clothes and fitted helmets on their heads. That done, Beauremon made his way to the biplane and climbed in, followed by the other. When they were settled in their places Gonzalez started the engine, and immediately there sounded a terrific roar as the Gnome barked out and the great propeller whirled.

San and Gonzalez held the machine until Beauremon gave the sign to let go, then the biplane shot ahead quickly, running along over the long stretch of level ground until Beauremon tilted the lifting planes. She answered immediately, and like a great bird shot upwards with incomparable grace.

Setting her to climb in a wide, sweeping circle, Beauremon settled in his seat, and from time to time glanced down at the water below, which was slipping away beneath them at the rate of seventy miles an hour.

Wu Ling, looking like some yellow sphinx from the past, sat motionless in his seat, his eyes fixed straight ahead and his arms crossed. For all the emotion his features displayed he might have been hammering along Piccadilly in a taxi instead of sweeping through the air at a terrific speed.

By the time the biplane had made a complete circle, bringing her nose back to the east, they had climbed to the two thousand foot level, and now, directly below them, the blue water of the Bristol Channel twinkled beneath the morning sun.

Far to the left the rugged line of the Welsh hills showed misty blue and black; to the right stretched the ramparted coast of North Devon; while behind them lay St. George's Channel, which broke on the coasts of Ireland.

The day itself gave promise of being perfect. Not a cloud flecked the unfathomable blue above, and at the two thousand foot level the soft August breeze caught them caressingly. It was an ideal day for flying.

Beauremon set the cloche for a very gradual climb, and picking out two tiny patches of black smoke, which came from steamers far below, steered a course midway between them.

At three thousand feet Beauremon set his right foot forward on the steering-bar, and ever so gradually the huge biplane swung southwards. Still she was climbing, and by the time they were at the four thousand foot level she was heading due south with eighty miles an hour being ticked off on the speed indicator.

Suddenly, far, far below them, a small dark blotch appeared. It looked like nothing so much as a dirty grey chip floating in a wide basin of blue, but when they had drawn almost directly over it, Wu Ling leaned forward, and, cupping his hands, shouted:

"Lundy Island!"

Beauremon nodded, and drew back his foot a little. The biplane swerved eastward again and swung along until Wu Ling again leaned forward and pointed down.

"There!" he called.

Beauremon looked over the side. The distant Welsh coast now only showed as a dark line to the north. The coast of North Devon was immediately beneath them, and where the sea broke against it there showed a long line of white.

Gauging the shore-line with a careful eye, Beauremon tilted the planes and set the biplane to descend in a long volplane. At two thousand feet he shut off the engine, and, shifting the rudder-bar a little, took the descent in a gradual spiral.

Lower and lower they dropped until the beach below seemed to fairly fly to meet them, then as it became still more distinct, Beauremon headed for a wide part which lay glistening white beneath the sun. The nose of the biplane came round slowly as they spiralled, then they slid towards the landing spot; the wheels touched the sand, there was a slight shock as the skids took the ground and they ran along easily to stop just where a tiny sand dune rose. It was a perfect descent and a faultless landing.

For a few moments after the machine came to a stop both Beauremon and Wu Ling kept their seats, gazing up and down the beach. They fully expected some wandering fisherman to come along and gaze with wonder at the strange machine which had dropped from the sky, but at the end of a quarter of an hour there was still no signs of anyone, so they descended and stood on the sand by the biplane.

Beauremon drew out his watch, and, turning to Wu Ling, said:

"We were wise to come early. It is only ten minutes to six now, and it looks as if we had managed to come down without being seen. I was certain the coastguards would see us."

Wu Ling shrugged.

"They may have done so, and even if they have, what care we? I have seen to all that. I have papers in my pocket which will serve to lull the suspicions of any coastguards. But come, let us wheel the machine along to the spot I have chosen in which to conceal it. Your landing has brought us less than a hundred yards from it."

They both took hold of the biplane, and, turning it, began to trundle it along the beach until they came to a thick patch of wood. There Wu Ling made a sign, and after a close scrutiny of the beach, they ran the machine in under the cover of the trees. Nor did they stop until they had succeeded in thrusting it into a deep tangle of cover which would have hidden two machines. And there Wu Ling showed how carefully he had planned things.

"I have been in Cardiff for weeks," he said, as they sat on the ground beneath the machine. "I came over here several times in a motor-boat, and after choosing this spot, set about to prepare it for the reception of an aeroplane, for I knew that if this affair was to be brought off it could only be done so by the air. I'll wager no passing coastguard will discover this spot. It will be uncomfortable remaining in this wood for two days, but the prize is worth it. We have sufficient food and drink, and can manage to amuse ourselves in some way."

Beauremon smiled.

"We shall manage all right," he replied. "Our man comes down to-night, doesn't he?"

Wu Ling nodded.

"Yes. To-morrow he will be playing on the links close by, and we may get a chance then to get him. If not, we shall have to try Sunday. I have here a plan of the links, and in your spare time you can study it."

So Beauremon, with that cool insouciance which was such a deeply-ingrained quality of his nature, lighted a cigarette and proceeded to study the plan of the golf-links which Wu Ling gave him. And the Celestial! What of him? Squatting on the ground he turned his gaze towards the sea, and for hour after hour sat there like a yellow sphinx, calm, all knowing, and inscrutable.

All that day did this oddly-assorted couple sit there in concealment, but in the evening Beauremon slipped off his flying clothes, and making his way to the sea bathed his face and hands in the cool brine.

Then he walked along the beach until he came to the village of Westward Ho! where he struck off across country. He kept on until he reached Northam, and, following Wu Ling's instructions, took the road leading to the residence of Mr. Grindley Morrison, one of the big land holders of the district and a former member of Parliament. It was this place which Wu Ling had said the Munitions Minister would visit.

There Beauremon lay concealed, until late that same evening a powerful motor-car drove along the road and stopped before the main gates of the place. While it waited for the gates to be opened, Beauremon slipped along in the shadow, and by the reflected glow of the powerful road lamps caught a glimpse of the occupants.

Then as it drove up the long approach to the house he started back for Westward Ho! well pleased with the result ofhis scouting mission. He had seen the Munitions Minister in that car.

The next day Beauremon and Wu Ling lay concealed in the wood close to the golf-links, watching, watching always for the opportunity they sought. Hours went by. During the morning they saw the Munitions Minister and another gentleman playing a round, but on that occasion no opportunity presented itself to put into operation their plan.

In the afternoon the same thing occurred, but so closely guarded was the Minister that they were compelled to return to their place of hiding that evening without having made a move.

Sunday morning they were once more on the spot, but the conditions were even worse than they had been the day before. Instead of two men, four were playing, and when after lunch the same thing occurred, it began to look as if all their efforts were to be crowned by nothing but rank failure. Still they lay there, watching like hawks for their prey to come within reach, and after tea on Sunday afternoon their chance came.

The Munitions Minister came in sight, swinging one of his golf clubs and smiling softly to himself at the result of a particularly fine drive which he had made from the fifteenth hole. Far in the distance the watchers could see another figure topping the rise, which they recognised as the man who had been with the Minister constantly, and who Beauremon knew to be Sir Hector Amworth, the head of Amworth, Strong & Co., the great heavy gun makers.

They watched closely while the Munitions Minister, who was carrying his own bag of clubs, selected another club, and approached the spot where his ball lay.

It brought him less than twenty yards from the spot where Wu Ling and Beauremon lay concealed. From there they could see that it was a brassie which he had chosen, and Beauremon, holding up a cautioning hand, peered out while the Munitions Minister raised the club to strike the ball. Then, half-rising, the baron opened his lips, and, in a somewhat muffled voice, called:

"Help! Help!"

They saw the Munitions Minister pause even as the club was above his shoulder and listen. Again Beauremon called, this time in a tone even more muffled than before, and then they saw the Munitions Minister turn and look towards the wood where they lay.

The next moment he had shouted something at the top of his lungs to his distant companion, and, turning, raced towards the spot from which the cry had come. As he did so, Beauremon and Wu Ling rose, and, as the Munitions Minister dashed into the wood, they both launched themselves at him.

Now, while by no means a powerful man, the Munitions Minister was lithe and active and full of courage. The moment the two men sprang at him, he saw the trap which had been laid for him; but, determined not to be overpowered without a struggle, he raised the brassie which he still carried, and, as Beauremon came at him, struck out with all his force.

There was a cracking sound as the blow got home, and the next moment the club snapped in half as the blood poured from a deep wound in Beauremon's forehead.

The baron staggered, and, had the Munitions Minister taken to his heels, he might even then have escaped. But, instead, he turned to meet Wu Ling's attack, and, as the Celestial struck him, the pair went down together. The Munitions Minister just had time to call for help to the companion whom he knew must be near, and then Wu Ling's fingers closed on his throat.

Beauremon, who had recovered a little from the blow which he been dealt, also took a hand, and, picking up the Minister, they carried him through the wood towards the beach. At that same moment, the Munitions Minister's companion dashed into the wood, and, leaving the Minister to Wu Ling, the baron crouched to wait for him.

Sir Hector Amworth came on at full-speed, and, as he passed the tree where Beauremon crouched, the latter sprang, clubbing a heavy revolver as he did so. The next moment Sir Hector Amworth lay full-length on the ground, unconscious. Taking him by the shoulders, Beauremon dragged him towards the beach, and left him close to the wood while he went along after Wu Ling.

The Chinese prince had carried the Munitions Minister to a spot just opposite, where the biplane lay concealed. There Beauremon lent him a hand, and together they conveyed the now unconscious Minister to the biplane.

They dumped him into the cockpit unceremoniously, and returned for the other. He shared the same fate, and then the two daring men—one the product of the mysterious and inscrutable Orient, the other the child of an effete Occident—trundled the great passenger-carrying biplane out to the beach.

Climbing in, Beauremon turned the rear starter, and Wu Ling, who had clambered in after the baron, had just time to sink down in his seat, when, with a roar, the machine started along the beach. A moment later she was mounting, while the water slipped by underneath at seventy miles an hour.

And the only person who saw the exact spot from which the biplane rose was a single boy, who was idling about some distance along the beach.

End of Prologue

CHAPTER 1.   The Missing Minister—Blake Called In.

"The Minister of Munitions has disappeared, Blake!"

Sexton Blake gazed thoughtfully out of the window, which looked from the private room of Sir John—, Chief of the British Secret Service, on to a flagged and cemented courtyard, but vouchsafed no remark.

"The Minister of Munitions has disappeared," repeated Sir John, "and, Blake, he must be found without delay!"

Blake nodded, but still remained silent.

"I have got together the facts which are actually known, and have cut out all the theories, of which there have been plenty," continued the chief. "Listen, and I will tell you what is known. On Friday evening the Minister left town in the company of Sir Hector Amworth, of Amworth, Strong & Co., the big munition people. Their destination was Westward Ho! on the north coast of Devon. As you know, the Munitions Minister is fond of golf, and while he is under such a pressure of work it is practically his only relaxation.

"It was their intention to play golf over the week-end, and to return to town last evening by car. Instead of arriving here Sunday evening, as intended, they have not put in an appearance up to now, and, as you see by the clock, it is half-past eleven. In half an hour it will be midday Monday.

"In ordinary times it would be just possible that the Minister might remain over longer than he intended, but certain extremely important matters demanded his presence in town by midnight Sunday.

"One of his secretaries waited up all night for the car to arrive, but when it did not come he got on the phone to the house at Northam, where the Munitions Minister and Sir Hector were staying. The result of that telephone conversation caused him to come hot-foot to me. This is what he told me:

"It seems that the Munitions Minister and Sir Hector Amworth arrived in Northam, which, as you know, is very close to Westward Ho! on Friday night, about ten o'clock. I may say that the Press was not cognisant of their destination when they left town. It was merely given out that the Munitions Minister was leaving town for the week-end, therefore unauthorised persons could hardly have known his intentions.

"At Northam they were guests of Mr. Grindley Morrison, the former member from that district, with whom the Munitions Minister is very friendly. It was he to whom the secretary spoke on the 'phone. The Munitions Minister and Sir Hector retired early Friday night, and breakfasted early Saturday morning.

"They motored through the Westward Ho! golf links a little after nine, played golf till noon, lunched at the hotel at Westward Ho! and continued their game during the afternoon. They returned to the house in Northam in time for tea, and spent the rest of the day within the grounds of the Morrison place.

"Sunday morning they again motored through to the links, and this time Mr. Grindley Morrison and a neighbour, Major Colin Hart, went with them. They played a foursome during the morning, which the Munitions Minister and Major Hart won. Then they went on to the hotel for lunch, and played another foursome during the afternoon.

"The car had been sent back to the house in Northam for a hamper, and they had tea on the links. After tea, Mr. Grindley Morrison and Major Hart remained at the club-house while the Munitions Minister and Sir Hector Amworth played round for a small wager. After the sixth hole they disappeared from view, and no more was seen of them.

"Time went on, and the two gentlemen who had remained at the club-house thought the game was taking a long time, but never dreamed that anything might be wrong. They attributed the delay to lost balls. I should mention that no caddie accompanied the players, since it was Sunday, and the Munitions Minister would not have one on that day.

"At last, however, it got so late that Mr. Grindley Morrison and Major Hart both became slightly worried. They decided to walk out to the eighteenth hole, and work back along the links from there, thinking they would pick up the players about the sixteenth or seventeenth hole. They did so, but worked clear back to the ninth hole without seeing the slightest sign of the players. I believe you know Westward Ho! links, Blake?"

Blake nodded.

"I have played there often, Sir John."

"Then you will know the topography of the golf links there, and will be able to follow intelligently what I have told you. You will remember that the links are situated on Braunton Burrows, on the seashore, and overlook Bideford Bay. You will also be familiar with the position of the different holes, and in your mind can follow the course of Mr. Grindley Morrison and Major Hart as they walked from the eighteenth hole in search of the missing players.

"As I have said, they reached the ninth hole without seeing any signs of them, and not until then did they become really worried at their absence from the scene. They consulted as to what they should do, and Major Hart suggested that they retrace their footsteps to the sixteenth hole, which, it seems, is close to a small wood, which lies between it and the sea.

"They thought the players might have suspended the game for a little to walk through the wood to the seashore in order to admire the view. The two searchers followed this plan, and made their way back to the sixteenth hole. From that green they turned off towards the wood, and, entering it, followed a path which led to the shore.

"About half-way along this path they suddenly came upon a golf-bag containing several clubs, and on the ground beside the bag was the lower half of a driver. The upper half of the handle-shaft they found some distance on. It had been broken, as though under force of a blow, and both bag and clubs they recognised as belonging to the Munitions Minister.

"By now keenly exercised in mind, they followed the path to the sand dunes on the shore, and there found a second bag with all the clubs intact. Mr. Grindley Morrison identified it as the one belonging to Sir Hector Amworth. Close to the bag there seemed to be the marks of several footprints, but so confused were they that nothing could be made of them.

"They went up and down the beach for the best part of an hour, shouting and halloing at the top of their voices, but gained no reply. Thinking, perhaps the two missing men might have returned to the club-house, and anxious to get an explanation of the reason for the two bags of clubs being where they were, they hurried back across the links, carrying the bags with them.

"On their arrival at the club-house, they called the steward and questioned him, but he was positive in his statement that neither of the gentlemen referred to had returned. You can imagine the state of mind in which Mr. Grindley Morrison and Major Hart now were.

"It had dawned upon them that something of a very serious nature had transpired, and, realising the importance to the country of those two gentlemen, set out again to make a thorough search. They went from one end of the links to the other, searching and calling, and not until they reached the tenth green did they hear anything which might by any chance throw any light on the occurrence.

"There they came upon one of the caddies, who had heard their shouts. He said he had spent the afternoon down by the military school, and had seen nothing of the two men for whom his questioners were searching. But he added that late in the afternoon he had seen an aeroplane leave the beach far up past the golf links, and that it had flown in a northerly direction.

"If there had been an aeroplane near the links, it would not be odd that anyone at the club-house should not hear it, for, if you remember, there is a long pebble beach at Westward Ho! which, when the tide is coming in or retreating, makes a loud, booming noise which would effectively drown the noise of an aeroplane engine at that distance.

"As it happened on Sunday, it was high-water at five-thirty, so the booming of the pebbles would continue for the better part of the afternoon, and—so the Munitions Minister's secretary says—Mr. Grindley Morrison informed them it was particularly loud that day.

"Mystified by what the caddie had told them, they walked along the beach to where he had seen the aeroplane rise. There they searched about until they found what may have been marks made by the wheels of a machine as it ran ahead to rise, but they could not make sure. They thought the lad must be romancing, and questioned him closely, but they could not shake his story.

"They sent for Mr. Grindley Morrison's chauffeur, and pressed him into the search. They covered every yard of the links and beach, and made an examination of all the bits of wood which are about there, but the result of all their efforts was nil. There was only a slight hope that the two missing men might have returned to Northam.

"While rather a far-fetched theory, it was always a possibility that a message had come to Northam for the Minister of Munitions, and that his own chauffeur had brought it out to the links. From the road he would follow, he might see them playing and might have taken it direct to the Munitions Minister without the formality of first taking it to the club-house.

"Presuming this, and further presuming that it had been an urgent communication, it is just possible, though, I confess, not probable, that the Munitions Minister and Sir Hector decided to abandon their game, and return at once to Northam without waiting to notify the others of their intention.

"But on the arrival of Mr. Grindley Morrison and Major Hart at Northam, they found that even this hope ended in thin air. No message had come for the Minister of Munitions, nor had anything been seen of either him or Sir Hector. The chauffeur was in the garage with the car, and had heard nothing from his master.

"Mr. Grindley Morrison and Major Hart at once sent word to a few gentlemen in the neighbourhood, men whose discretion they could depend upon. They held a meeting in the library of the Morrison place, where Mr. Grindley Morrison told them what had occurred. Then they formed search-parties and searched the whole night. Mr. Grindley Morrison had just returned to the house, and was deciding that he should notify London of the mysterious disappearance, when the secretary of the Munitions Minister got through to him.

"That is the whole story as I have had it from the secretary, and he gave it to me as he got it from Mr. Grindley Morrison. Of course, you can readily see, Blake, what a serious thing this double disappearance is. To-day, the Minister of Munitions was to meet a very important deputation from several of the producing firms of the country. This evening he was due for a Cabinet conference. To-morrow he had another important conference on, and was on Wednesday to speak in Birmingham on munitions.

"In addition to those engagements, there is much urgent matter in his department which will of necessity be hung up during his absence. He is the brains and driving force of that end of things, and without him business will be almost entirely suspended. A message has been sent to the deputation which was to wait on him to-day, telling them that important business has made it impossible for him to keep the engagement, and postponing it until the end of the week.

"The Prime Minister has been told the truth, and he at once sent for me. He has impressed it upon me that we must find him without delay. His disappearance from the scene of action will cause tremendous complications. The other engagements he had, will, as far as possible, be filled by his assistants, but it is he himself who is necessary. That is all I can tell you, and the rest you must find out for yourself. You can work out the problem in your own way, only find the Munitions Minister as quickly as possible—much depends on it. Will you take up the matter, and push it forward without delay?"

"Of course, I will do what I can." responded Blake, rising. "I shall go to work on the matter at once. You are sure there is nothing further I can learn in London about this affair? Do you think the secretary could give me any further facts?"

"I don't think so," replied Sir John. "I questioned him very closely, and what I have told you is everything I elicited from him."

"Very well, I shall go to the scene of the disappearance and start to work there," said Blake.

With that he picked up his hat and stick, and shaking hands with the Secret Service Chief, strode towards the door. He passed through several corridors, and between several police guards, until he reached the lift, and entering it, was taken down to the ground floor. Passing out into Whitehall, he entered the big car, which, with Tinker at the wheel, was waiting for him.

"Drive to Baker Street at once," he ordered, and Tinker, turning slowly, sent the car along Whitehall at a good pace.

Crossing Trafalgar Square, he drove along Regent Street to Oxford Circus and there headed for Portman Square and Baker Street. He drew up in front of the house in Baker Street, and at a word from Blake followed his master into the house. Once in the consulting-room Blake tossed aside his hat and stick, and lit a cigarette.

"Sit down, my lad. I wish to speak to you," he said.

Tinker threw his cap on a table and sat down.

"Something serious—something very serious has happened, Tinker," began Blake. "The Minister of Munitions and Sir Hector Amworth have both disappeared while playing golf on Westward Ho! golf links. As far as is known, these are the details of the affair."

Forthwith he began and repeated to Tinker the story Sir John had told him. When he had finished, he said:

"It would only be a waste of time to theorise now. We must get to the spot without delay and see what we can. I must confess that, so far, the aeroplane spoken of by the caddie is the most suspicious circumstance, but on investigation that may prove to be nothing of importance. But we shall go prepared for all eventualities.

"In this case speed is the chief requirement. Therefore, you will get a taxi and drive through to Hendon. Telephone the mechanics before you go. Tell them to get the Grey Panther out and get her tuned up.

"When you get to Hendon, you will get into the Grey Panther and start for Devon. Come to earth as near to the Westward Ho! golf links as possible. If you take note of the western end of the golf course, you will find a very decent landing-place close to the beach.

"Myself, I shall drive down in the car and meet you there. Don't wait for lunch, but take some sandwiches and a Thermos flask with you. With luck you should arrive at Westward Ho! before me. If you have to come to earth some distance away, get some reliable men to look after the Grey Panther, and come on to the links. That is all. Now lose no time."

Almost before Blake finished speaking, Tinker was making for the telephone, and, ringing up the hangar at Hendon, spoke to the mechanic, telling him to get the Grey Panther ready at once for a flight. Then replacing the receiver he caught up his cap, and with a nod to Blake hurried out.

Blake, on his part, went into his dressing-room, and threw a few things into a bag. Then opening the door he called to Pedro. With the big fellow trotting at his heels, he made for the street and entered the car. A few moments later, he was thundering along Baker Street, heading for the surburbs and the open country, along the road to the west.

He stopped once on the way long enough to send a wire to Mr. Grindley Morrison, warning him of his coming, and then once he had struck the open country, he let out the throttle and sent the car ahead at a terrific pace.

Through Middlesex he went across a point of Surrey into Berks, and thence he traversed Wilts, until he crossed the border into Somerset. From Somerset he took the direct road to Taunton, and pausing at Taunton long enough for some hasty refreshments, continued his way into Devon, heading for Barnstaple.

At Barnstaple he stopped for five minutes, replenishing his petrol, and seeing to his lights, then on to Northam, only a few miles distant.

At the old sleepy town of Northam, which, in the days of Drake and Hawkins, was, with Appledore and Bideford, a place of bustle and excitement, as the cargoes from Virginia came up the bay and entered the Torridge, Blake paused to ask the way to the Morrison place, then on again to where it lay—a huge black pile of Tudor lines set in the heart of an ancient park, which had gathered vigour from the breath of the sea.

He drew up at the gates, and while waiting for the lodgekeeper to open them, glanced at his watch. It was just on nine o'clock, so that to come from Baker Street to the gates had taken him just under eight hours—not bad, considering the distance was over two hundred miles.[1]

When the gates had been opened he drove up the long, tree-lined driveway which led to the house, and when through the deepening night he saw the picturesque house, he noticed that the windows were thrown open to the warm August night, and caught sight of the white gleam of shirtfronts on the verandah in front. He drew up near the side entrance, and leaping from the car, ran up the steps where a man in dinner-jacket stood waiting to receive him.

He put out his hand as Blake reached the top and said:

"You are Mr. Blake, I presume? Ah! Now that I see your features, I recognise you. I am Grindley Morrison. I received your wire early this afternoon, and have been anxiously awaiting your arrival."

"Then there is still no news?" inquired Blake, as he shook hands and removed his motoring-cap to allow the cool night air to refresh him.

Morrison shook his head.

"Not a sign of them. But come along and have some supper. I will tell you all I can then."

Taking Blake by the arm, he led him into the main hall of the place where a footman relieved him of his dusty coat. Then when he had washed, he followed his host to the room where supper had been spread. At a word from Morrison, the servant who was in attendance retired, and when the door had closed after him Morrison said:

"Go ahead, Mr. Blake. You must be famished. I will talk while you eat."

Blake set himself to investigate the merits of the several dishes which had been prepared, for in truth he was hungry, and while he ate the other talked. He repeated, more or less, the story which Blake had already had from the lips of the Secret Service Chief. When he had reached the point where he had received the 'phone message from London, he paused for a moment to take a sip of port, then proceeded:

---

[1] Without accounting for stops, that is 25 mph! /drf

20

"Needless to say, we have searched all day. Several of my neighbours have joined in the search, and though our efforts must have aroused some curiosity, I am certain nothing definite is suspected, for the Munitions Minister was here incog., and no one knew he was to be my guest. I was at Westward Ho! when your telegram was brought to me, and as you requested in it, I kept a sharp look-out for an aeroplane. But during this afternoon none appeared."

"That is rather odd," interrupted Blake. "My assistant was to leave London about two this afternoon, and flying at the speed he would, he should have not take more than four hours for the journey. What time did you leave the links?"

"Not until dusk set in. Some of the party have remained at the links, but when I left, no aeroplane had shown up, and although I left word for a message to be sent on to me in case one did, none has come. If there had been any news I should have heard without delay. I came on here to meet you, but was afraid you would not arrive before ten o'clock at the earliest."

Blake tapped the table thoughtfully.

"I cannot understand why Tinker has not arrived. He should have been here. However, he may have had engine trouble on the way, and it may have been necessary for him to come to earth somewhere. If that is the case, he will hardly attempt to finish the journey to-night, but will wait until morning. Now, if you are agreeable, I should like to motor over to Westward Ho! and have a look round."

"Certainly, Mr. Blake. I am entirely at your service. I realise only too well what a serious matter this is, and the fact that both gentlemen were my guests, makes me feel it all the more keenly. But I can't for the life of me imagine what has happened. What could happen to those two in broad daylight on a golf links? I know, of course, that their absence from the helm would complicate matters vastly, and would grant a valuable delay to the enemy, but who would have dared to carry out such a thing? And yet, there must have been foul play."

Blake rose and lighted a cigarette.

"Surmise at present is useless," he said. "When we have had a chance to view what slight evidence there appears to be, and have collected that evidence together, then, and only then, may we attempt to form some theory as to what happened. By the way, where are the two golf-bags?"

"I have them in my study," replied Morrison. "Do you wish to see them?"

"When we return," said Blake. "If you are ready, I think we had better be getting along."

They left the room and passed out to the hall, where a man brought their coats and caps. They made their way outside, where Blake's car still panted at the steps. As they reached the top of the bank which rose from the driveway a man came towards them, and when he had drawn nearer, Blake saw that he was an elderly individual, with the stamp of the retired military man about him. He was therefore not surprised when Morrison introduced him as Major Hart, who had been a member of the golfing party when the mysterious disappearance took place.

He accepted Blake's invitation to join them, and, taking the wheel, Blake turned the car and started down the drive. On reaching the main gates he turned to the left, and with the powerful road-lamps picking out the road which wound like a white ribbon over a mantle of sable, they raced for Westward Ho!

Blake, who had often played on the Westward Ho! links and accounted them among the finest in all Europe, knew the way perfectly, nor did he slacken the pace until the car had passed the hotel and was skirting the links.

Instead of driving on to the club-house he kept on to the beach, from which came the boom, boom, boom of the great pebbles as the receding tide ground them viciously together. Here he drove more slowly until, at a word from Morrison, he drew up and all three descended.

"This is where we started the search," remarked Morrison, when they had alighted. "I suppose you will want to start here, too. We should meet some of the other searchers at any moment."

Blake dug beneath the rear seat of the car and produced a powerful acetylene lamp, which he turned on and lighted. Then he spoke:

"If you will lead the way, Mr. Morrison, I will follow. I do not know that I care to spend much time here. I wish to go chiefly to the spot where the caddie says he saw an aeroplane rise."

Morrison grunted, and, turning, led the way over the sand dunes along the beach until the lights of the village dropped behind, and only the incessant booming of the sea on the pebbles filled the night. To the right shone the light on Bideford Bar, while now and then as they topped a dune they could catch a glimpse of the revolving light on the southern point of Lundy Island, which stands sentinel at the gaping mouth of the channel.

Far up the shore they came upon two men, who were standing close to the water gazing out to sea. They turned as Blake and his two companions appeared, and by the light of the acetylene lamp he carried, Blake could see that they were both rather elderly.

Morrison introduced them as two neighbours, and when they were informed of Blake's name, they gave him an account of the evening's search. They told a tale of woods searched and shore examined foot by foot, without any signs of the two missing men. Blake listened to their report, then, thanking them, requested Morrison to show him the exact spot where the aeroplane had been seen to rise.

Morrison led the way into a near-by wood, and, making a circuitous way to the shore again, paused between two sand dunes.

"It was here," he announced.

Blake, holding the lamp so that the flare would fall on the sand, dropped to his knees and began to make an examination. It was not difficult for him to locate the two lines which Morrison attributed to the wheels of an aeroplane, and at the end of a few minutes Blake was strongly inclined to agree with him.

But to make a detailed investigation of the marks that night was out of the question. Though the acetylene lamp was powerful, still it would not show up the faint marks which might be there and on which Blake might find reason to hang his chief theory.

But now he had located the spot and could gain some idea of it's topography in relation to the lie of the shore and the sweep of the channel, he could apply his intelligence with more certainty to the evidence which had been related to him by Sir John— and endorsed by Morrison that same evening.

When he had risen to his feet he closed the mask of the lamp, and addressed the four men who stood close at hand.

"Gentlemen," he said, in low tones, "it must be quite evident to all of you that this affair is of a most serious nature. It must further be plain to you that for the present, at least, the truth must not leak out. Mr. Morrison has vouched for your discretion, and when you understand that matters vital to the safety of the nation are involved, you will see why nothing must be said. Therefore, I want you all to pledge your word of honour that until permission is given you, you will say nothing about this."

A deep rumble of voices answered Blake as each one of the quartette gave his word. Then Blake resumed.

"With the gentlemen who live in the district, and who have already been taken into Mr. Morrison's confidence, we should have a sufficient force to keep guard here and watch for any development at this end. The line from here shall be in my own care. But for the present, at least, it will be necessary to preserve every atom of evidence until I can make a thorough examination of it. Therefore I want you to volunteer to take turns guarding the spot. Will you volunteer?"

It was Morrison who answered.

"I can speak for all of us here, as well as the others, who are at present about the links somewhere. We are only too keen to do all we can, and you may consider us, one and all, under orders, Mr. Blake."

Blake bowed his thanks.

"How many of you are there?" he asked.

Morrison thought for a moment, then said:

"Seven."

"Then I think it would be a good idea to divide the force up into watches. If three watches of two each were formed that would take six, and you, Mr. Morrison, could superintend the matter. In that way we could guarantee that this spot and a certain portion of the links would be under continual surveillance for the next few days, which may be critical. On the other hand, if we are successful in our efforts it may only be necessary for me to ask the services of yourself and your friends for a day."

"I shall certainly arrange to do this, Mr. Blake! We will pick up the others and arrange the first watch."

Here Major Hart spoke up.

"If one of you gentlemen," he said, referring to the two whom they had found on the edge of the shore, "will volunteer for the first watch, I will also do duty."

Immediately one of the pair volunteered, and they took up their places by the spot where the aeroplane was supposed to have risen. Then Morrison struck off across the links to acquaint the other three men with the new arrangements, and Blake, well satisfied that the spot would be well guarded until daylight, when he could make a

24

proper examination of any evidence there might be, returned to the car and waited for Morrison to come up. In about ten minutes he appeared, and, climbing in, said:

"I have fixed things up. The others are arranging the watches and will snatch some sleep at the hotel while they are not on duty. I shall return about midnight to see how they are getting along."

Blake nodded, and, starting the car, drove back to Northam. Arriving there he drove to the Morrison garage, where a man took charge of the car, and following his host into the house, went along to the study where the two golf-bags which belonged to the missing men had been taken.

The bag which Sir Hector Amworth had carried presented no particular features of interest. It was a well-made canvas bag, having a hood which protected the clubs. Blake unfastened this hood and examined the clubs one by one, but beyond revealing the ordinary signs of wear, he received no suggestion from them.

Laying this bag aside he picked up the one which had been carried by the Minister of Munitions. It was a very handsome bag of pigskin, well fitted with protecting hood of the same material which fastened by a patent lock, as did the other bag.

In addition, it was provided with all the accessories desired by the inveterate golf player—ball pocket, sponge pocket, umbrella holder, and a multiplicity of leather straps and other fixtures.

On raising the hood Blake saw that it was packed with all sorts of clubs from drivers—of which there were three sorts—to cleeks and putters, the latter represented by two designs.

It was the bag of the enthusiast who knew his game. Taking out the clubs one by one, Blake made a cursory examination of them and laid them aside. At last there was only one left in the bag, a finely-balanced mashie, which he laid beside the others before thrusting his hand into the bag to see what else was there. Then he came upon two broken pieces, one of which Morrison had picked up in the wood and the other on the beach.

Now Blake laid the bag aside, and carrying the broken club closer to the light concentrated his attention first on the shaft. He saw that it had been broken almost exactly midway between the top of the shaft and the tip of the club. It was a brassie, well made and strong, and as he gazed upon the clean break, Blake knew only a heavy blow could have caused it.

He put aside the top part of the shaft and picked up the club end. This he studied for some time, then thrusting his hand in his pocket, drew out a powerful pocket-glass which he applied to the examination.

Along the lower edge of the brassie's face he had seen something which had aroused his curiosity, and now through the glass he made out that the marks which had attracted him were neither the stains made by grass nor yet the remains of mud. They were tiny spots mostly, with one fairly large blotch about the size of a threepenny-bit—dark brown in colour and possessing no lustre.

Blake puzzled over the marks for some little time before suddenly he shot forth his hand and between his fingers carefully grasped something which had been adhering to the lower part of the club. Then as he held his hand up to the light, Morrison, who had been watching closely, saw that he held in his fingers a short hair. Blake laid down the club and placed the hair under the glass.

For some minutes he studied it; then raising his head, he said:

"This is an important discovery, Mr. Morrison. There can be no doubt but that this is a human hair, and unless I am greatly mistaken we shall find when I have made a thorough test that the stain on the lower edge of the face of this brassie is human blood. In my opinion, the club was broken owing to the violence with which a blow was dealt with it.

"Good heavens!" exclaimed Morrison. "Do you think that is the hair and those stains the blood of the Munitions Minister?"

"That is, of course, impossible to say; but hazarding a guess, I should think not. It is more likely to be the trophies of a blow which he dealt his assailants, for that there were assailants seems a certainty now. No, I should much prefer to think that they were the results of a struggle, in which the Munitions Minister had used the first weapon which came to hand and which he was probably holding when the attack came. Though how it came or whence, we cannot guess.

"But to-morrow I shall make certain tests and prove whether or no this is human blood and if this is a human hair, although I am fairly certain on the point already. Whoever wielded this club dealt a fierce blow, and I do not envy the man who received it on his head.

"Now I think that is all we can do to-night, Mr. Morrison, and if you do not mind, I shall retire. I will take this club with me. If anything comes from Westward Ho! please call me at once."

"I will do so," replied Morrison. "I am going out there at midnight to see how things are going on, but unless there is something important to report I shall not wake you."

Blake thanked him, and saying good-night, left the room. He went at once to the room which had been assigned to him, and, carefully laying the broken pieces of the brassie on a table, began to undress. He spent little time in futile theorising, but slipped into bed, and, although worrying a good deal over Tinker's non-appearance, soon drifted into sleep.

It seemed to him that he had scarcely dozed off when he was awakened by a furious pounding on his door, and sitting up in bed with a start, became aware that Morrison was outside the door shouting:

"Wake up Mr. Blake! I have just had a message from the links. There is an aeroplane wheeling round and round overhead, as though looking for a landing-place!"

CHAPTER 2   How Tinker Brought the Grey Panther to Devon

When Blake had counted on four hours as being good flying time for Tinker to get from Hendon to Westward Ho! he had calculated conservatively. With favourable conditions the journey could be made in a machine like the Grey Panther in something under that time. But neither Blake nor Tinker were able to anticipate the trouble which the lad was to have.

When Tinker left Baker Street he hailed a taxi and drove straight through to Hendon. There at the hangar, which Blake used for the Grey Panther, he found that the mechanics had already wheeled out the slim shape of the monoplane.

She stood just without the hangar, shining beneath the warm afternoon sun, her lines as slim as those of any bird, and her silent Gnome engine sufficient in itself to suggest the lure of the boundless azure above. Sexton Blake had designed well when he designed the Grey Panther.

Tinker spent some twenty minutes examining the struts and stays and in tuning up the engine, then, climbing into the cockpit, he gave the word to the two mechanics, and, as the engine roared out and the propellor spun, they released her and she ran ahead in a straight line, throbbing beneath the reserve power of the engine.

A slight lift of the lifting planes and she rose easily; a pressure on the rudder bar and she swung to the left, picking out a spiral course which would take her to the two thousand foot level in a wide swing having a diameter of several miles.

Then Tinker settled back in his seat in full accord with the perfection of movement, which the Grey Panther at all times achieved.

Up, up, up she climbed, until the blunt nose of the Grey Panther pointed west, then, releasing the slight pressure of his foot on the rudder, Tinker let her forge ahead.

Catching the straight bend of the air, the monoplane quivered like a nervous horse at the start of a race, then the ground below was sweeping away beneath with the dark smudge of buildings growing less and less clear as the green country beyond was reached.

Mile after mile was ticked off with swift regularity. Towns were sighted, passed and left behind in a patch of grey and black. Villages and hamlets swept into view and were lost again. A lone farm here

28

and there, the spire of an ivy-covered church, an occasional motor far below on a narrow country road, a slow moving farm cart, a solitary man in one of the fields which formed part of a widely-spread draughtboard—all these and the hundred and one details which the airman sees, passed beneath them as the Grey Panther swept on her way.

Over county after county until he was over Stroud, in Gloucester, went Tinker, then he headed for the wide mouth of the Severn and the Bristol Channel. Away beneath soon glistened and reflected the long line of rocks and sand bars which stretched away to right and left until they broke into the shores of South Wales and North Devon respectively.

As he sighted them, Tinker made a mental calculation. He knew that if he kept straight on down channel, making Lundy Island his point of direction, he would eventually come opposite Westward Ho!—which was his destination. By following a straight line in this fashion he would have the broad line of the channel to guide him, and when opposite Westward Ho! a slight turn to the left would fetch him towards the land.

With this intention, he let the monoplane keep her present direction, and in the ordinary course of events, he would undoubtedly have fetched his landing place. But when the converging upper part of the channel had been left far behind and only the widening sweep of the blue water could be seen, he suddenly sat up in his seat and gazed away to the north, where a dark speck had appeared.

At first it looked like a bird wheeling high up against the blue sky, but as he continued to gaze at it Tinker knew it was no bird, but an aeroplane.

Hastily he swung the chart-stand towards him and gazed at the map of West of England which he had affixed before leaving Hendon. Then, looking to the north, he saw that the other machine was climbing high and heading westward.

"She is from Cardiff way," he muttered; "or, if she is not from Cardiff, she has been flying in that vicinity. I wonder if she is from an air station on the South Wales coast? I'll shift my course a point and see if I can pick her up. Might have a little race down Channel."

Suiting the action to the word, he put his foot on the rudder-bar and gave a slight pressure. The monoplane answered smoothly, and the next moment they were sweeping along on a different course—a course which, while it was still westward, would bring them in gradually until they were closer to the strange machine which Tinker reckoned was now about three thousand feet up. Incidentally, he shifted his lifting-planes a trifle, intending to climb to the level of the other machine.

Slowly the form of the other became more distinct. In another ten minutes Tinker saw that she was a biplane, and then a little later his eyes widened a trifle as he made out the full strength of her lines.

"Thunder!" he muttered. "She is certainly some biplane—a passenger machine, and big at that. I wonder where she is making for? Anyway, the Grey Panther has more speed, and I should be able to overhaul her soon."

During the last few miles Tinker had felt that bane of all airmen—air-sleepiness. On a warm day, with a machine running easily and little wind to strain at the stays, an airman is almost certain to fall under this species of air hypnotism, and in more cases than one it has been the death of those who have yielded to it.

Therefore, the lad more than welcomed the opportunity of a race, for it would rouse all his faculties, keeping him on the alert each moment.

Whether the pilot of the other machine had seen him or not he could not say. In any event he had so far paid no attention to the slim shape of the monoplane which was coming up behind him, and with a superb disdain of the Grey Panther, was forging away westward.

Tinker smiled to himself as he viewed the wide spread of the biplane, then, pressing the accelerator of the monoplane, he sent her leaping ahead. The speed indicator climbed from seventy to eighty miles an hour, from eighty to eighty-five, then to eighty-seven, and, at that Tinker let her hum.

The nearer he drew to the biplane, the more he became impressed with her great size and power, though in a straightaway race she would be no match for the slim and speedy monoplane which Blake had built.

By now the Bristol Channel stretched away on either side until the land was only a dim line north and south, and getting less clear each moment. Then the biplane ahead altered her course a trifle, heading more to the north in a direction which would bring her closer to the Welsh coast.

Tinker gave his rudder-bar a pressure and followed. As the Grey

Panther came round he saw that the pilot in the biplane had taken sufficient notice of him to increase his speed, for now the big machine shot ahead at a swifter pace with the monoplane gaining very little.

"At last he has decided to race," chuckled the lad. "It has taken him long enough to make up his mind. Well, we will give him a pretty little run of it until we get opposite Westward Ho! The way he is going now he will drag me across the channel to the Welsh coast, but it won't take long to cross back again."

But Tinker was to find that the big biplane could kick out more speed than he thought, for now she increased her pace again, and for a short time the Grey Panther dropped back. Not until he had sent the speed-indicator up to ninety-five miles an hour did he start to gain again, and then, absorbed in the progress of the race, he did not notice that already he was far down channel.

Not until there suddenly appeared below him a long line of breakers, whose shock was taken by high and jagged cliffs, did he realise that not only had he passed the point which would be opposite Westward Ho! but had got far out towards St. George's Channel.

"Those must be the cliffs of Pembrokeshire," he muttered. "We have certainly come along some. I didn't realise how fast we were eating up space. I guess I had better turn back and call it an unfinished race. Perhaps I'll meet you again Mr. Biplane and give you a better run for your money."

As he pressed his foot against the rudder-bar to make the turning, he leaned over and gazed down at the sea below. He could see the ragged-looking line of coast with a myriad small islets thrown off from it, and in some cases almost hidden by the flying foam as the waves rolled in and broke upon them in a shower of irridescent spray. Between them and the narrow patches of sea which separated from the mainland, Tinker could see the white gleam of low-lying sands and the water glistening on vicious and wicked-looking rocks, bare and gaunt at low tide, but swept by a swirling mass of green and black as the water rose.

Jammed in between them he could, in imagination, see the narrow guts and crevices in which the tossing water sucked and whirled, meaning death to the strongest swimmer were he caught within them. Then, far to the north, away by itself, was one islet larger than those immediately below him. It stuck out, gaunt and bare-looking, from the height at which he viewed it, and for all the world looked like a great solid stone triangle dropped in the sea by one of the mythical giants of old, or a chosen spot on which Neptune or Thetis might rest while viewing the tossing waves which they ruled.

For miles he had scarcely moved the cloche or foot-bar, but now, as he started to turn and while still gazing away at the other machine, his foot suddenly caught in a wire leading to the switch, and in a moment he had pulled the connection loose. The next second the motor stopped, and, after the barest of quivering pauses, the monoplane plunged downwards.

It was fortunate for Tinker in that moment that he was up almost three thousand feet. Had he been only a few hundred feet in the air he would have had extreme difficulty in managing the machine for the drop, but long experience had taught him instinctively what to do, and while getting the Grey Panther into the correct angle for the volplane, he reached down and tried to catch hold of the wire end and replace it on the binding post.

No use!

Try as he would he could not reach it. It waggled aggravatingly just out of reach of his fingers, and straightening up he looked over the side.

"Nothing for it but to let her continue on the volplane and find a place to land," he muttered. "And what a place to have to come down. I haven't the floats on to-day, so can't come down on the water. Nor does there seem to be a square foot of level ground about those cliffs or islets, let alone a flat stretch where I could come to earth with an aeroplane.

At that moment his eyes lit on the triangular-shaped island which lay beyond the small group of islets below him.

With a quick glance he took in the details of the level surface which it presented, and saw that, contrary to what he had thought when at three thousand foot level, there were buildings upon it. Only two houses could he make out to be sure, but that meant people and people meant help in an emergency.

Then his eyes caught the sight of the great biplane dropping earthwards, and to his amazement, he saw that she was volplaning towards the island. Then every atom of his attention was needed for the Grey Panther.

He was about eighteen hundred feet above the sea now, and calculated swiftly that a direct volplane would carry him some distance beyond the island.

Jamming his foot against the rudder bar he changed the course of the machine and sent her into a spiralling volplane which would bring him down on the island. Then, bracing tight, he watched every movement of the Grey Panther, ready for any emergency which might occur.

He was not alarmed at the predicament in which he had managed to get himself. Had there not been a possible landing on the small triangular-shaped island he would have been in a very unenviable position, but the closer he got to earth the better he liked the look of the landing; and, if he could direct the volplane correctly, he would be little worse off. It would take him very few moments to replace the end of the wire on the binding post and then he could get away again.

Now he saw that the biplane, instead of landing on the island, had started her engine again and was rising in a spiral, but he saw at the same moment something white drop from her and float downwards towards the island.

From one of the houses two men ran out, and Tinker had just time to see that they were making for the spot where the white article must fall, when a patch of wood hid them from view, and all his faculties were taken up with making a landing.

The monoplane came down easily, and, striking the ground with her skids ran ahead and stopped with scarcely a jar.

After the barest look round at his surroundings, which he saw to hold little attraction, Tinker bent down, and, catching the end of the wire, fixed it to the binding post.

Then he screwed up the nut which held in its place, and, straightening up, prepared to get out. He knew just beyond the wood by which he had come down he would find the houses; and it was his intention to seek aid of the two men he had seen run out from one of the buildings.

But scarcely had his foot touched the ground when from somewhere in the wood there came the sound of a rifle, and the next thing a bullet plunked through one wing of the monoplane, just whizzing past Tinker's head.

Tinker whirled quickly and gave a loud "Hallo!"

"Look out there!" he yelled.

For answer the rifle barked out again; and this time a bullet passed through the arm of his coat to strike the Gnome, and ricochet from it to the ground by the lad's feet.

"This is a little too hot for comfort," he muttered, gazing in amazement at the spot from which the shots had come. "Those shots could hardly have come as close to me by mere accident. Hallo!" This as another shot struck the tail of the machine.

With that Tinker leaped into the cockpit, and, bending towards the rear starter, gave it a turn.

Just as the engine roared out, two men burst from the cover of the wood and started to run towards him. One of them stopped after a few yards; and, raising a rifle to his shoulder, fired. The bullet whistled over Tinker's head, and, ducking, he bent low while the Grey Panther tore along the stretch of level ground.

The men who, where they stood, were on his left ran on a little further, then both of them stopped and began firing at him. The bullets tore through the thin wing material of the monoplane and went ripping past the lad's head but no real hit was registered, and a few moments later, when the monoplane had gathered sufficient headway for a rise, Tinker shifted the lifting planes and sent her up.

But not yet did the fusillade of lead stop. All the time he was climbing to the thousand foot level they followed him, nor did they desist until the spiralling course he was following had taken him well out of range.

Then, as he pressed the rudder bar and sent the Grey Panther round to head towards the Bristol Channel, he saw, less than a mile distant, the huge biplane which, in the first instance, had been the cause of his getting so far away from his intended destination.

Tinker reckoned she was about on the two thousand foot level, and as he gazed at her he was puzzled by her movements. She was wheeling round and round in narrow circles, banking at dangerously steep angles as she turned and, seemingly, flying aimlessly.

Putting two and two together, however, it was not difficult for him to guess what was her purpose. He remembered how she had volplaned down towards the island while he himself was dropping. He recalled, too, the white article which had dropped earthwards from her, and which the two men had run from the house to get. Then he called to mind how a vicious and murderous attack upon himself had immediately followed.

Now the biplane was wheeling about watching for him. He was certain of it. Yet it puzzled him, even as he pressed the accelerator, to figure out why this should be so. When he had first sighted the big biplane back Cardiff way he had changed his course a point with the intention of having a friendly race down channel.

Although he did not recognise the machine, he reckoned she was one of the new craft of the extended air service, and, knowing the type of aviator in the ordinary British machine, he did not anticipate for a moment that his challenge would be refused.

Following that, the biplane had increased her speed and they had raced westwards. Then, when the accident had occurred to the Grey Panther, Tinker had found himself over a rocky portion of the Pembrokeshire coast. And yet, in thinking over the race, he recollected that the biplane had always been ahead, thus setting the pace and thus choosing the direction.

It was because he had followed her that he had reached such a lonely spot as he had. But that did not explain the reason for the white article which had been dropped from the biplane to the island, and which, in Tinker's opinion, had caused an unwarranted attack to be made upon him.

Only his own rapidity of action had saved him from being drilled by several bullets. Why? That was the puzzle. Nor was he left long in doubt as to the intentions of the other machine.

As the Grey Panther turned her nose towards the east, Tinker saw the biplane swing after him and drop to the two thousand foot level on which the monoplane was now running.

Had Blake been with him, or had he not been bound under sealed orders, he would have felt strongly inclined to trust to the speed of the Grey Panther in order to circle round and spend more time in the vicinity in an endeavour to discover the reason for what had occurred.

But, realising that he was already well behind time, and that Blake would expect to find him at Westward Ho! when he arrived, Tinker decided to make a run for it and to leave the mystery to the solving of the sea birds.

The biplane, however, evidently had no intention that he should get away, for it now tore after him, and, coming at a sharp angle, made a strong bid to cut him off, while from the cockpit there followed a perfect hail of bullets as someone in the biplane opened fire on him.

Tinker settled in his seat and gazed straight ahead, while the speed of the monoplane gradually climbed from seventy-three to eighty miles and then from eighty miles to ninety.

At that he left it, and, as the sea swept along beneath him, he took the opportunity to turn and look back. The biplane was steadily dropping away behind him, and, when twenty minutes later he looked again, he saw that she had disappeared from view. He was just congratulating himself that he had shown a clean pair of heels to the other, when there was a sudden stoppage of the Gnome, followed by a loud explosion as she back-fired. She picked up again a moment later, but before another minute had passed she stopped once more, repeating her back-fire.

Tinker eased his pressure on the accelerator, and, setting her at a slight angle, let her volplane down to the thousand foot level. At the same time he peered anxiously to right and left where the dim line of shore loomed.

He judged he was a trifle nearer the coast of North Devon than that of Wales, and as the Gnome picked up again he pressed the rudder bar with his foot and pointed the nose of the Grey Panther towards the right.

It was only by the most persistent nursing on his part that the Gnome consented to run, and then the action was intermittent and irritating. Still he held on, and, as the line of shore became more and more distinct, he sought anxiously for a landing spot.

A little later he descried a patch of white, which later resolved itself into the village of Clovelly, which nestles in a cut in the cliffs in the lee of Hartland Point.

Then he knew exactly where he was, but seek as he would he could find no spot where he could land. With the engine still running badly he circled out to sea again, the diameter of his sweep taking him in the direction of Lundy Island, which sits bleak and lonely at the mouth of Bristol Channel, sixteen miles from Hartland Point.

Mile after mile was ticked off with the Gnome spluttering and complaining, then, when he had climbed to the two thousand foot level for safety, and when Lundy lay off to the right, the Gnome gave another loud explosion and stopped entirely.

Setting the planes at the angle for a spiralling volplane, Tinker let the monoplane drop in a sweep, which he hoped would fetch the island. He knew that on the flat surface of Lundy there would be little difficulty in finding a landing spot.

Down to the thousand foot level the Grey Panther dropped, then swept in a spiral to the five hundred, and, with a gentle sweep, soared down to a flat stretch close to a wide-mouthed quarry where Tinker could pick out the white patches of upturned faces.

Then the skids touched ground, and Tinker was just about to give a sign of relief at having found a landing place when, for the second time that day, things went wrong; for without the slightest warning, the monoplane heeled over, and as her right wing struck the ground there was an ominous crash.

A strut had smashed. Nor was it until an hour later that Tinker discovered the reason. The spot where he had landed was in a direct line with a deep cut through the quarry which opened straight through to the sea. This cutting formed a vast sort of chimney which caught up the air by the sea and drew it through to the other end of the quarry in a never ending gale of wind.

The monoplane had come athwart this, and as the blast of wind had caught her she had tripped up.

She stopped with the crash, and Tinker leapt to the ground. Immediately several husky looking men ran out of the quarry towards him, and, as they drew near Tinker, who was now suspicious of everything and everybody, saw with relief that their attitude was friendly.

He knew that Lundy Island was owned privately; and that almost the only thing it produced was stone. These men, he thought, must be employed by the owner to quarry the stone, and a few moments later he found that to be so.

They paused by the machine, and in rough but kindly Devon dialect offered to do what they could to help him. Most of them had never seen an aeroplane before, and were lost in wonderment while Tinker good-naturedly explained how it worked.

They had not yet reached the point where they could look on it as anything else but an uncanny creation to be regarded from a safe distance.

When he had gone over the different parts and demonstrated briefly the science of flight of heavier-than-air machines, Tinker set himself to go over the engine and find out what had caused it to behave as it had.

It took him a solid hour to locate the trouble; and when he did he found it was a leakage in one of the valves. That meant the valve must be removed and ground, which, would consume at least another hour.

With the assistance of some of the men from the quarry he set to work, and in the blacksmith's shop attached to the quarry, managed to get the valve into working order again. Then he was compelled to turn his attention to the damaged strut which he found to be a much more serious break than he had at first thought.

Darkness fell and found him still working away at it, and not until the evening was well advanced was he able to assure himself that it was repaired as well as possible.

Then he decided on a thing which only the most daring of aviators would have considered. He determined, in spite of the fact that it was past ten o'clock and full night, to risk flying towards Westward Ho! trusting to the distant light on Bideford Bar to guide his direction and to the revolving light on Lundy, with the small beacon at Clovelly, to assist him in keeping his course.

The quarrymen tried their best to dissuade him, but the lad persisted, and while several of them held the Grey Panther, Tinker started the engine.

The Gnome roared out and then purred smoothly.

Tinker clambered in and gave the word to release her. The monoplane ran ahead, and a few minutes later, with the lifting planes canted, she started to rise.

With his eyes straining ahead through the night Tinker settled down and set the nose of the machine for Bideford Bar Light, knowing that once he had reached that vicinity he would be practically at Westward Ho! And on the chance of finding Blake at that place depended his chances of making a night landing.

So the Grey Panther raced on, with Lundy dropping steadily behind.

CHAPTER 3   Blake Fulfils His Commission

When Blake was awakened by Mr. Grindley Morrison and informed that a message had come through from Westward Ho! saying there was an aeroplane circling overhead, his first thought was of Tinker.

As he slipped into some clothes he puzzled over the circumstances, wondering why, if it were the lad, he was doing dangerous night flying. Then he remembered the other machine, whose traces had been left on the beach by the golf links, and the thought came to him that perhaps it might be that one.

If so, why had she flown over in the night to circle above the spot where the Munitions Minister had been kidnapped?

When he opened the door and went out into the passage he found Morrison standing at the head of the stairs waiting for him.

"Now then!" said Blake briskly, as they went down the stairs together. "Have you any details?"

Morrison shook his head.

"No; only the bare message, saying that there is an aeroplane circling overhead at a considerable height. I took the liberty of telling my man to get your car ready. I took it for granted that you would want to go to Westward Ho![2] at once."

Blake nodded his thanks, and pausing in the lower hall long enough to get a cap and motoring coat, they hurried outside to the garage. The big grey car was standing just within the door with the engine purring softly and the road-lamps already turned on. Blake climbed in followed by Mr. Morrison, and then the car leaped ahead and started down the drive towards the main gateway.

Once in the road Blake let her out, and they ticked off the few miles to Westward Ho! in record speed. Just as they reached the road by the lower side of the golf links Blake glanced up, and far overhead was able to make out a peculiar yellow and red glow.

---

[2] 'Royal North Devon at Westward Ho! can rightly claim to be the cradle of English Golf. Founded in 1864, it is the oldest golf course in the country and is regarded as the St Andrews of the South. The golf course is as tough as any of the UK's more famous links layouts and has recently been placed in Golf World 's "Top 100 Courses in the World" that a golfer "must play".' From their website /drf

He knew at once that it could only come from the exhaust of an aeroplane and as he brought the car to a stop, shutting off the engine, he could distinctly hear the steady drone of an engine up above. By the glow of the exhaust he could follow her course, and, watching her as she flew, he saw that she was going in a wide circle above the links.

He stood rigid for a few moments, listening to every shade of tone of the engine; then turned to Morrison.

"It is my own monoplane," he said briefly. "I could recognise the song of her engine in any place. For some reason my assistant has risked a night flight, and is circling above until we line out a landing place for him. We shall have to work carefully, for a descent to-night will be a risky business."

Morrison glanced upwards and whistled softly.

"He has a nerve!" he muttered. "How will you arrange a landing-place Mr. Blake?"

Blake did not reply for a moment. Instead, he gazed ahead into the gloom which masked the stretch of the beach from view. Finally he said:

"Will you go on and get the two men who are on watch? Have them pull a quantity of the long, dry grass which grows close to the edge of the beach. We shall need a fairly large quantity. In the meantime, I shall be arranging other matters."

Morrison puzzled at Blake's request, but obediently hurried away to carry out the instructions, while Blake returned to the car.

Climbing in, he drove slowly along the beach until he reached a spot which he remembered from the day. He knew that from there the beach stretched away flat and hard for some distance until it broke against a small sand dune just opposite the spot where he had seen the marks left by the aeroplane which they supposed had been used by the kidnappers of the Munitions Minister.

There he stopped, and getting out, switched out the lights of the car. He waited a moment then switched them on again, leaving them thus for a minute. Again he doused them, turning them on again, and for a third time extinguished them for a minute. Then he turned them on and let them burn in all their brilliancy, with their powerful rays sweeping along the straight run of the beach. He had thrown a triple signal to the machine overhead, and if the aviator were on watch he must have seen it.

A moment later Morrison appeared followed by two other figures. All three carried huge armfuls of dry grass, and, under Blake's direction, they placed in several small piles along both sides of the beach, one line following the line of the water and the other following the line of the underbrush.

When the first lot had been placed they returned for more, and then again for a third lot. When it had all been placed as Blake directed the line-out was thus. At the head of the long flat stretch of the beach the car, with the great road-lamps sweeping the full length and lighting it up was a white patch which could be plainly seen from above. Then on either side the piles of dry grass, placed at intervals of about ten yards the whole width of the beach between the lines.

Blake's next move was to tell off the two watchers to one side, while he and Morrison took the other. Then, when Blake gave the word, they started down the lines touching matches to the piles of grass as they ran.

Immediately the dry material flared up, and when all the piles had been lighted, Blake rushed back to the car and masked the lights once. Almost immediately there was a cessation of the drone overhead, and gazing upwards, they could see by following the glare of the exhaust that the aeroplane was volplaning.

Guided by the grass flares on the sides and the lights of the car at one end, the machine dropped swiftly until the watchers could distinctly make out her dark slim lines. Then she grew still more distinct, and a few minutes later had taken the beach at the far end from where the car stood, and was running along the blazing line of flares which Blake had caused to be lighted.

It came on easily until the drag of the skids on the sand gradually brought it to a stop, and at last she came to rest not ten yards from the road-lamps of the car. The next instant the grass flares died down and then became extinguished.

From the aeroplane, which the watchers could now see was a monoplane, a figure clambered out and came along the beach to meet them. Blake, who was in the lead, spoke as the figure approached.

"You made a splendid landing, my lad! But what possessed you to attempt such a risky landing by night?"

"I thought it was necessary, guv'nor," came a clear young voice in reply. "I have had it pretty warm since I left Hendon, and will tell you all about it."

He had reached the group by this time, and when Blake had introduced the lad to the other three gentlemen, he said: "Now then, Tinker, let me hear what has happened."

Tinker leaned against the mudguard of the car, and, beginning with his arrival at Hendon, related all that had occurred until he had decided to leave Lundy Island in spite of the darkness.

When he had finished there was a deep silence for some minutes, broken finally by Blake.

"Peculiar—very peculiar!" he murmured. "You say this big aeroplane had come from Cardiff way, my lad?"

"Yes, sir," replied Tinker—"at least, I should judge so from her direction."

"Do you think her course towards the west was impelled by your appearance?" continued Blake.

"No, sir; I do not. She was headed west when I first sighted her, and I think I saw her before her pilot saw me."

"What followed seems to bear you out," mused Blake aloud. "Following your story, it seems that she flew west until over the Pembrokeshire cliffs. There you had an accident with the wire connection of the motor and were compelled to seek a landing. She also volplaned down towards the one spot where you thought it safe to come to earth, but instead of landing, as you thought she would, she rose again after something had been dropped from her. This article fell on the ground near one of the houses, and just before the Grey Panther touched earth you saw two men run out and pick it up."

"Yes, sir."

"What was it like, my lad?"

"Well, guv'nor, I only caught a glimpse of it, but it looked like a small paper packet."

"Then a few minutes later there was a most murderous attack made upon you," went on Blake. "It would almost seem that it was the receipt of the packet dropped from the biplane which inspired this. Nor does there seem any doubt but that an attempt was made to kill you before you got away from the island. Had the accident to the motor been more serious, and had you been delayed, they would have succeeded in getting you. Then, when you rose you sighted the biplane circling round, and immediately she started in pursuit of you.

"As I remarked before, it is all very peculiar. It is hardly possible that those in the biplane would know your identity. Had any other machine followed them as you did, it seems that a similar attack would have been made upon them. That means it was not you who were attacked, but the one who drove a machine which had followed them. Meaning, I think, that they had some strong reasons for not wishing their movements to be known.

"Now, were it any Government machine they would not have made this attack without first ascertaining whether you were friend or foe. Such a thing would be against all the probabilities. Therefore, we may safely conclude that it was a private machine. But why—why should they have done this?"

"I can't imagine, guv'nor," muttered the lad. "When I sighted the machine I changed my course, in order to have a race down Channel. It was with no intention of following them, though, from my actions, it is possible they thought I was doing so. Anyway, they attacked me, as I have told you, and, if the Gray Panther had not been the faster machine, they would have brought me down even after I got away from the island."

Blake paced off to the edge of the water and stood gazing out to sea, thinking deeply. Five minutes went by and still he stood there, puzzling over the strange adventure the lad had had.

Finally, he turned to the others.

"We can do no more to-night, gentlemen," he said. "If you will continue to keep watch as before, I shall be greatly obliged to you. Mr. Morrison, I shall return to your place. Will you come?"

"I am at your service," responded Morrison.

"Come along, my lad," said Blake, turning to Tinker. "You must be badly in need of some rest. To-morrow we will discuss in detail this adventure of yours."

They climbed back into the car, and, backing her round, Blake started back towards Northam. Arriving there he drove the car into the garage, and, when Tinker had been shown to a room, bade good-night to Morrison.

He ascended to his own room, but not to retire. Instead, he drew up a chair by the open window, and, lighting a cigar, smoked in the darkness for a long time. Not until the east was greying did he rouse himself, and then it was to make his way to the bathroom for a cold plunge.

When he had shaved and dressed again he went along to Tinker's room and knocked up the lad, then descended to the lower hall to discover that Morrison was already abroad.

"I haven't slept a wink all night," he said, when he had greeted Blake. "This affair is nearly driving me crazy. I can't for the life of me think what has happened to the Minister of Munitions. And then there is the strange adventure your assistant had, though I don't suppose that had anything to do with the other. But, at the same time, I am certain the kidnapping was done by aeroplane."

Blake shrugged.

"It would be folly to try to connect the two events while we know so little," he said. "But, at the same time, there is a certain channel of investigation which it might pay to follow. I intend doing so to-day after another examination at Westward Ho! By the way, Mr. Morrison, have you a large scale-map of the Welsh coast?"

The other nodded.

"Yes, in the library. Do you wish to look at it?"

"If you please."

"Then come with me, Mr. Blake. You will have time before breakfast is served, though I have told them to hurry with it." They went along to the library where Morrison brought out a large map portfolio. In this Blake found the one for which he had asked, and, bending over it, examined it closely. He followed the line of the Pembrokeshire coast until he came to the myriad of small islets which lie near the extreme western point.

There he traced out the different names until he found the name of Marsey. He studied the location of this tiny spot on the map for some time, then finally raised his head.

"Thank you!" he said. "Shall we go to breakfast now? I think I hear the gong going."

They went out into the hall where they found Tinker waiting, and then on into the breakfast-room. They ate hurriedly and in silence, for each was busy with his own thoughts. After the meal they climbed into the car, and, with Blake at the wheel, drove to Westward Ho! There they descended and received the report from the two gentlemen who were then on duty.

Nothing else had occurred worth reporting since the arrival of the Grey Panther, and when he had listened to what they had to say Blake turned to Tinker.

"Come with me my lad. There is an examination I want to make."

He and Tinker went along together to the spot where Morrison had located the marks of an aeroplane, and in the clear morning light Blake made a thorough examination of the spot. Here and there he could make out the flat line of what he took to be the impression of a skid, and, following the wheel marks, traced them through the grass and bushes to a secluded spot in the wood beyond.

There he dropped to his knees, and, after a thorough examination of all the surrounding ground, rose, and spoke to Tinker.

"You say this biplane which you followed yesterday was exceptionally large, my lad?"

"Yes, guv'nor," replied the lad eagerly. "She was one of the biggest I have ever seen. I reckon she would carry four or five men easily. She wasn't as large as the 'bus Graham White built to carry six or eight men from London to Paris, but she would have run it a close second."

Blake nodded thoughtfully.

"Tell me, my lad," he said, after a little—"what do you think of these marks?"

"Well, guv'nor, they are pretty wide, and, from the depth of the skid marks, I should say the machine which made them was pretty heavily loaded."

"My opinion exactly, Tinker," replied Blake. "And if you will pace the width of the tire marks you will find that they are nearly a foot farther apart than the ordinary wheel marks of a biplane. What does that tell you?"

Tinker's eyes suddenly widened.

"Great Scott! Guv'nor, do you mean to say that these marks may have been made by the biplane I saw yesterday?"

Blake smiled.

"I would not go so far as to say that, my lad, but they were certainly made by a very large machine, and it was an exceptionally large machine you saw yesterday. We must remember that, as far as we know at present, only one person saw an aeroplane rise from this beach here on Sunday afternoon. That was a lad who was idling about the beach, and who on week days is a caddie at the golf course.

"From what he told Mr. Morrison, it seems that the aeroplane went in a northerly direction, and he would hardly have said that unless he had watched her out of sight. Now, by the time she would have been that distance away, she would be getting well over the Welsh coast, and, my lad, she would be only a short distance away from the triangular-shaped island where you came down, and which I have already identified on the map as Marsey Island off the coast of Pembrokeshire.

"Let us follow that theory a little. From what we have seen here, it seems safe to assume that the machine which left the Westward Ho! beach was of a size larger than ordinary. That, in turn, presupposes that she was a biplane. When she left here she was flying in a direction which would take her not far away from the Island of Marsey.

"Yesterday you met a biplane off the Welsh coast, and it, too, was a machine larger than the ordinary. In addition, the course it took brought it over the island of Marsey where the occupants made a communication of some sort to men on the island—a communication which was followed by an attack upon you.

"It may be only a coincidence, but, in my opinion, it is one worth following. It will be an extraordinary coincidence if we prove that those two over-size machines which were flying along the Welsh coast within a few hours of each other were not one and the same. So tune up the Grey Panther, my lad. We are going to make a flight to the island of Marsey."

Tinker, only too delighted to return to the island in Blake's company, pushed his way through the scrub, and raced along the beach towards the Grey Panther. Blake himself followed more leisurely, and when he appeared Mr. Grindley Morrison and three of the other gentlemen who had been patrolling the spot came to meet him.

To them Blake merely said that he was going off in the monoplane to follow a clue, and that, if all went well, he would return some time during the afternoon. Then they walked on to where the machine lay.

While Tinker tuned up the Gnome, Blake carefully examined the broken strut which the lad had fixed on Lundy Island; then, when the motor was humming soft and regular, Blake opened the locker in the cockpit and took out his flying clothes.

Slipping them on he donned his helmet, and climbed in. Tinker followed suit, and when they were settled in their places with Blake at the throttle, Tinker gave the word, and those who had been holding the Grey Panther released her.

She shot along the beach, then, as Blake tilted the lifting-planes, took the rise easily. Up she went, climbing in a wide spiral until they reached the thousand-foot level.

Blake pointed her blunt nose towards the north, and they shot away swiftly with the speed indicator creeping up from sixty to eighty-five.

Tinker, gazing back, saw the white spots which marked the upturned faces of those on the beach; then they were well out over the sea, with the distant shore rapidly becoming a white-rimmed line blurred and indistinct.

Blake settled in his seat, and not until the Welsh coast loomed up ahead did he alter his course. When the line of breakers grew fairly distinct, he shifted the direction a point, and away they went towards the west.

Mile after mile of the coast on their right passed away beneath them, and here and there a smudge of smoke appeared marking a steamer making her way up or down Channel. Then the jagged point of Pembrokeshire appeared, and a few moments later they came in sight of the tiny islets which lie off it.

Blake glanced once at his chart, then and again changed the direction of the Grey Panther. Just as he did so a small triangular patch appeared ahead, and in the reflecting-mirror Blake saw Tinker raise his hand, signifying that is was the same island where he had come to earth the day before.

Blake drove on only a short distance further before cutting off the motor, then, circling, he started on a steep volplane.

Down, down, down, they went in a long, slanting glide until the island which had been well ahead of them suddenly swept beneath them.

Down still more, until the buildings upon it became distinct, and the formation of the ground showed up plainly. Then the island seemed to leap to meet them, and, with a gentle shock, the Grey Panther touched earth on the same stretch of level ground where Tinker had landed.

No sooner had she run ahead and stopped than Blake rose, and dropped to the ground, followed by Tinker.

"Get your revolver out my lad!" ordered Blake curtly. "I didn't see anybody about as we came down, but our descent must have been witnessed, and, after your experience of yesterday, we can guess what sort of a reception we are likely to have."

Tinker nodded, and, removing his flying-helmet, drew his automatic. Then, when Blake had done likewise, they started off at a run towards the wood which separated them from the buildings which they had seen.

They entered the wood at the nearest point, and, pushing their way through, suddenly came out into another patch of open ground, across which was a low-built farm building. At the moment it seemed untenanted, so quiet was it, nor could they know that the farmer-tenant of the island had been sent to Fishguard by his employer on business, which would take him the best part of a week to get through.

They began to cross the patch of ground, and, as they topped a small rise, they caught sight of another building—a large bungalow which faced on the miniature bay which the island boasted.

No sooner had they done so than they discovered they were not to go ahead without their advance being opposed. They saw a door of the bungalow open, and two men step out on to the verandah.

Though Blake and Tinker were a considerable distance away, they were near enough to make out that both men carried rifles, and, even as they realised this, a bullet whizzed past Tinker's shoulder.

At a word from Blake, they dropped flat, taking their shelter behind the rise.

"They saw us, as I thought they would," said Blake. "We can never rush them from here while they hold rifles. Our revolvers will not carry far enough for that. We shall have to try strategy. But to get there I am determined.

"There is something very queer about this place! They make not the slightest attempt to discover our identity, but the moment we show up fire on us, proving they are determined to keep trespassers off at any price. If they were honest, they would not do such a thing. They would inquire first, and I have yet to know of any British law which permits the occupiers of a place to fire on trespasses without finding out their reasons for being there.

"And, even when you were in distress in the air, and were forced to descend at the first available spot, they fired upon you. We shall have to make a run for the wood, and work our way round through it until we get closer to the house. Then we may be able to slip up on them close enough to use our revolvers. Are you ready, my lad?"

"Yes, guv'nor. But look, guv'nor—look!"

"Where?" asked Blake quickly, as Tinker uttered the

exclamation.

"There—in that upper window, guv'nor! Do you see it?"

Blake raised himself a trifle, and, risking the bullets which began to fly close to him the minute he showed himself, he gazed at the upper window of the bungalow which Tinker had indicated. He was just in time to see something white waving from it, then it suddenly disappeared.

"It was a signal of sorts, Tinker," he said. "The more I see of this place, the less I like it. However, we shall know the mystery of the place before we leave it, or my name is not Sexton Blake."

Drawing back under the lip of the rise, behind which they had taken cover, Blake and Tinker crept back for some yards. Then, at a word from Blake, they rose and raced for the cover of the wood.

A perfect hail of bullets followed them, but at the distance the aim was uncertain, and they reached the shelter of the trees in safety. Turning there, they gazed back towards the bungalow, and as they did so saw one of the figures descend the steps and head for the wood.

Blake uttered a low exclamation.

"Do you see their game, my lad? That is proof that there are only two of them at the house. One is remaining there on guard, while the other hunts us out with his rifle. Follow me! We will see if we cannot match our wits against theirs. Easy does it!"

As he finished speaking, Blake turned, and, bending his head, started off through the trees, with Tinker close on his heels. Blake took the direction leading to the right, and, keeping always in mind the location of the bungalow, travelled in a wide circle, which would eventually bring them out near the building.

They were not near enough to the edge of the wood to see what had become of the man who had started out to hunt them down with his rifle, but they were building on the chance that he would think they had returned to the field where the Gray Panther had come down, and make for there. In that case, it would give them a chance to rush the house.

It seemed as long time to Tinker before Blake paused and held up his hand, but he knew from experience how perfect was Blake's woodsman's knowledge, and that his master had a perfect sense of location in the thickest of jungle. To him, therefore, the comparatively open wood in which they were presented no difficulties.

A few minutes later, after creeping along on hands and knees for some distance, they suddenly came out at the edge of the wood nearest the bungalow, and Tinker saw exactly how certain had been Blake's scouting.

The building was now less than a hundred yards away from them, and, instead of being in a line with the front balcony as before, they were now at the back, and as far as they could see there was no one on guard there.

After a cautious surveillance of the situation, Blake rose, and said in a whisper:

"My idea is to rush it, Tinker. If we go gently, we should be able to reach the rear without being seen unless the second man is hanging about the open ground somewhere. Once we have reached the house, we will make for the front, and try to get our man before he can use his rifle to any purpose. Do you get me?"

"Perfectly, guv'nor. When you give the word, I shall be at your heels."

Blake nodded, and, stepping out into the open, began to make for the rear of the house, with Tinker close behind. Yard after yard they covered, until they were over half-away across. Then Blake broke into an easy jog-trot, and Tinker did likewise.

They reached the rear safely, and without pausing Blake continued round the side towards the front. Just as he did so, there was a shout in the distance, and out of the corner of his eye Tinker saw a man burst forth from the wood and, kneeling down, place a rifle to his shoulder. It was the man who had been sent out to hunt them.

The next instant they had burst into view of the front balcony, and came full upon the second man, kneeling down with the muzzle of his rifle sweeping slowly back and forth.

As he heard them, he swung sharply and pulled the trigger. Tinker saw Blake stagger slightly, then recover and go on again. In the same instant Tinker raised his automatic, and, pointing it full at the man who knelt on the balcony, fired point-blank.

At the distance a miss was impossible. The bullet caught the man full in the shoulder, and sent him backwards with the force of the impact, but with an oath he regained his balance, and again pulled the trigger of the rifle.

The bullet zipped past Blake, struck the barrel of Tinker's automatic, and ricochetted through one of the windows of the bungalow.

50

Then Blake, firing from the hip as he went, rushed the balcony, and Tinker swarmed over the rail beside him.

Full upon the other man they leaped, all three going down with a crash. In less than a minute, Blake and Tinker had the fellow helpless, and as they straightened up, Blake a low whistle of amazement.

The man's hat had fallen off in the struggle, and now he lay on his back with his face turned upwards to the full light of morning. It was this full view of the prostrate man's features which had inspired Blake's whistle of surprise.

"So," he murmured softly, "it is Gonzalez! Take a look at him, Tinker!"

Tinker was already doing so, and as Blake spoke he turned quickly.

"Gonzalez, of the Council of Eleven, guv'nor!" he exclaimed.

Blake nodded slowly.

"It is he. Secure him well, my lad! It is a little plainer to me now why trespassers upon this land are fired upon without first being challenged."

Scarcely had Blake given the order to Tinker, when from behind them sounded the sharp crack of a rifle, and at almost the same instant a bullet thudded into the railing of the balcony not six inches from the spot where Blake was leaning.

Like a flash Blake ducked, and, seizing the rifle which had been used by Gonzalez, he swung round, placing it to his shoulder as he did so. Across the stretch of open ground, close to the edge of the wood, he saw the figure of a man kneeling with a rifle at his shoulder, and just a puff of smoke came from it.

Blake pulled the trigger of the one he held. He saw the man by the wood fall forward on his face just as the bullet tore its way through the sleeve of his coat. Then, with a word to watch Gonzalez, he vaulted over the rail of the balcony, and carrying the rifle with him, started to run towards the spot where the other had fallen.

As he approached nearer, Blake raised his weapon ready for instant use. The little time he had been on the island had served to make him cautious, and though it looked as if he had registered a full hit, he knew that the prostrate attitude of the man by the wood might only be a blind to draw him on.

As he got still closer, however, he was able to make out the rifle of the fellow lying several feet away, and in the other's attitude there was an odd twist which seemed to indicate a complete prostration of muscular volition.

A few yards farther, and Blake dropped all caution, running forward until he was close beside the other. Then, for the second time within the space of a few minutes, he received a severe shock, for the man who lay sprawling forward on his face was not only not a stranger to Blake, but he was not a whiteman.

In him Blake recognised San, the famous lieutenant of Prince Wu Ling, of the Brotherhood of the Yellow Beetle. He did not pause then to puzzle out why San the Celestial and Gonzalez aviator, of the Council of Eleven, should be together on that tiny island off the Pembrokeshire coast. He saw a splash of deep crimson on the throat of the prostrate Chinaman, and, dropping to his knees, turned him over.

San's eyes were closed, and his breathing was short and laboured. He gave no sign as Blake moved him, and it was plain that he was unconscious, or nearly so. Blake passed his hand over San's throat, and as he wiped away the blood, came upon the wound which the rifle had made.

It had caught San on one side of the throat, just missing the jugular vein, and, ploughing its way along the soft flesh of the neck had finished up by striking the jaw-bone just beneath one ear—the reason, Blake imagined, why San was unconscious from the shock. The tiniest fraction of an inch more, and the bullet would have plunged through his jugular vein as potently as the knife of a pig-sticker.

Blake drew his handkerchief and mopped up the flow of blood, but even as he did so it gushed forth afresh, and he saw that unless San were to bleed to death in a few minutes he must use more efficacious measures. So, heavy though the Celestial was, he threw him over his shoulder, and started back towards the house with him.

Arriving at the balcony, he found Tinker standing guard over the Spaniard, whom he had also taken the precaution to bind securely. His eyes widened as he saw the identity of Blake's burden. He made no remark, but followed his master into the house, where, in a large and well-furnished living-room, Blake laid his captive on a couch.

Then together they found their way to the kitchen, where they procured water and towels, and with these returned to the living-room.

Setting to work, Blake bathed San's wound, and when the flow of blood had been stopped bound it up roughly but well. Then he signed to Tinker to tie the Celestial's hands and ankles, for, though San might be wounded, Blake knew of old the cunning and capability of the Oriental, and had no intention of taking any chances.

After that they dragged Gonzalez into the living-room, and, leaving him in a corner, proceeded to make a thorough search of the place. On the ground floor they found nothing, but neither of them had forgotten that white signal which had been waved from an upper window; so, when they had finished the lower floor, they made for the floor above.

The first room to which they came was a large bedroom which showed signs of recent occupation, but at present held nothing of interest to them. The second door was locked, and pausing before it, Blake knocked sharply. There was no summons in reply, but on the other side of the door they could hear a thumping sound which sounded like nothing so much a boot heel being pounded upon the floor.

That was sufficient for Blake.

Stepping back a pace he turned slightly, then rushed the door, catching it full with his shoulder. It crashed inwards with a rending and splintering of wood, and as they followed it into the room, they brought up to regard a strange sight.

Lying on the floor, bound and gagged, and presenting every sign of woe-begone discomfort, were two men dressed in golfing garb, and one of them—he who lay nearest the wall—Blake recognised as the Minister of Munitions, who had disappeared from Westward Ho! golf links a few days previously.

The trail of the big biplane had led them straight to the spot.

While Blake knelt and loosed the bonds of the man who meant so much to Britain, Tinker released the second man and the two got stiffly to their feet. Then the Munitions Minister, aching though he must have been in every joint, turned to Blake and said, with a faint twinkle in his eyes:

"Our last interview, Mr. Blake, was under somewhat different circumstances. Nevertheless, I am more than pleased to see you. Permit me to introduce you to Sir Hector Amworth."

Blake, catching the spirit of the Munitions Minister's unquenchable courage, smiled and bowed to the big gunmaker, who held out his hand.

Then, in a serious tone, the Munitions Minister went on: "How did you come, Blake? By boat? and have you raked in the rascals who did this?"

Blake shook his head.

"We have captured two of them, sir, but the real authors of the affair are not here. We did not come by boat, but by aeroplane. But come below, and I will see if we can get together something to brace you up. While you have some food, I will tell you all about it."

The Minister nodded, and followed by the others, made his way below. There Tinker exercised his ingenuity in preparing a hasty though nourishing meal for the two released captives, and while they consumed it, Blake related all that had happened since he had been sent for in London by Sir John—

When he had finished the Munitions Minister frowned.

"Then, you think, Blake, that the affair is due to the work of these two organisations of which you speak—the Council of Eleven and the Brotherhood of the Yellow Beetle? I, of course, know of Prince Wu Ling, through the other affair some little time ago, when the Crown Prince of Germany dared to come to England. But I cannot fathom why they should have joined hands for such a purpose as they attempted to carry out. And, certainly, our fate was already sealed. Last night a man came to see us, a tall, well set up fair man, who, from what you have told me, I judge was this Baron de Beauremon. He told us coolly enough that within forty-eight hours we should be killed, and that our bodies would be sunk in the sea. Then all day we heard nor saw nothing of them.

"The first signs we had that there was something afoot in our favour was when we heard the rifle shots. I managed to make my way to the window which I broke by banging my head against it. Then I got my teeth on Amworth's handkerchief and pulled it from his pocket. In this way I managed to wave it from the window, hoping it would be seen. But I was unable to keep it up for long. The attitude was too much of a strain.

"Then we heard more shots, and, as you know, you came soon after to find us. I cannot imagine what has become of the two arch scoundrels."

Blake shrugged his shoulders.

"The big biplane, which was the real clue in the affair, is not on the island," he said. "Undoubtedly they have gone away to arrange the details of their next move. It is probable that they will return some time to-day to put into execution their threat against you; and then we shall try to gather them in.

"But you, sir, I imagine, will want to get away as quickly as possible. The Grey Panther, unfortunately, will not carry more than two—one besides the driver. Therefore, I shall have to take you first, and return for Sir Hector Amworth. Tinker can remain here with him.

"Also, when I have dropped you at Westward Ho! I shall bring back a man with me to go on guard here, and wait for the return of the biplane. Then I can take Sir Hector Amworth to Westward Ho! and when I return for Tinker, bring back another man to go on guard with the first one.

"In the meantime you might arrange, sir, for a gunboat, or T.B.D. to put in here, and take off the two prisoners we already have. If it reaches here before the return of the biplane, it will come in useful in gathering in the pair who are the real authors of the outrage upon you. How does my plan strike you, sir?"

The Minister of Munitions accepted one of Blake's proffered cigarettes, and when he had lit it said: "Like all you do, Blake, it strikes me as being splendid. I do not think we can improve on those plans. What do you say, Amworth?"

Sir Hector nodded.

"I agree with you," he replied. "I think we had better place ourselves entirely in Mr. Blake's hands."

"Then, if that is agreed upon, we will get away as soon as you are ready, sir," said Blake to the Munitions Minister. "Time will be of value; and besides, London will be wondering what has become of you."

The Munitions Minister smiled as he rose. "It will simply be told that I remained a day or two longer at Westward Ho! than I intended," he said. "Anyway, I had the satisfaction of striking one good blow at the scoundrel who attacked me."

"It was a very powerful blow," remarked Blake, rising also. "It broke the brassie as clean as could be."

The Munitions Minister paused and gazed at Blake in astonishment. "How on earth did you know that?" he exclaimed. It was Blake's turn to smile.

"That was not difficult." he said. And with that enigmatical reply he led the way outside.

On the way through the living-room, the Munitions Minister and Sir Hector paused a moment to regard the two prisoners, then continued on their way. They walked across the patch of open ground to the wood, and pushing through it kept on to the spot where the Grey Panther lay.

While Blake tuned up the engine, Tinker and Sir Hector held the machine, and the Munitions Minister climbed in. When he had shaken hands with Sir Hector, and spoken a few words of thanks to Tinker, promising the lad to thank him properly in London he sat back, and Blake took his place. Then, with the Gnome singing sweetly, they ran ahead and rose easily.

At the two thousand foot level, Blake turned the nose of the Grey Panther south, and away they went at eighty miles an hour towards Westward Ho! Soon, far beneath them, the white line of beach came into view, and Blake shut off the engine and volplaned down, landing with scarcely a shock on the spot where Tinker had come to earth the night before. Then, as Mr. Grindley Morrison and several other gentlemen appeared, the Munitions Minister climbed out and received their congratulations.

Through his influence, a couple of men were sent from the nearest coastguards-station to return to the island, and leaving one of them on the beach to await his return with Sir Hector Amworth, Blake took the other with him.

The Grey Panther rose from the beach in a steep climb and tore away on her return journey to Marsey Island, with Blake giving her every bit she would take.

It seemed no time before the risky islets of Pembrokeshire appeared again, and when he had volplaned down to the triangular shaped island, Blake found Tinker and Sir Hector waiting for them. There the coastguardsman climbed out and Sir Hector took his place. Then, once more, the Grey Panther tore away and shortly after was once again circling over Westward Ho! for the volplane.

When Sir Hector had joined the Munitions Minister and the other gentlemen, who had been waiting at the club house on the golf links, Blake took in the other coastguardsman and started back for Marsey Island on his last journey. There he left the second man to join his mate, and after giving them full instructions as to what to do, he took in Tinker and began the return journey.

When they reached Westward Ho! again, they found that preparations were all completed for the Munitions Minister and Sir Hector Amworth to motor through to London at once. Before departing, the Munitions Minister took Blake aside and said: "Things are too pressing for me to thank you properly for what you have done, Blake. I shall do that in London. I have sent a message which will have a T.B.D. at Marsey Island within an hour. It will land a few men and remain in the vicinity. When the biplane returns, it will endeavour to gather in the two men we are after."

"That will be splendid," rejoined Blake.

Then he gazed thoughtfully out at sea.

"They are cunning, sir—none more cunning in all Europe than they. I have a feeling that I should return there and take a hand."

The Munitions Minister laid a hand on his shoulder. "You will do nothing of the sort, Blake. You have done in one day more than the whole police force of the country could have done in a week. Leave the capture of those two to the men who have been sent to get them. Return to London and rest easy—they must be taken."

"I shall do so, but I have been up against those same two more than once in the past, and I know what they are," said Blake. "However, we shall hope for the best."

So, shaking hands with the Munitions Minister and Sir Hector Amworth, he saw them into their car, and with Tinker at his side walked across to his own. He waited for Mr. Grindley Morrison to join them, and when he had done so, they motored back to Northam where they had a late lunch.

Then Blake got his bag and bidding good-bye to Morrison, they returned to Westward Ho! from where Tinker was to take the Grey Panther back to Hendon.

When the lad had risen and was flying easily at the two thousand foot level, Blake climbed back into the car and started for London. He drove at a stiff pace through Devon and Somerset, for he was anxious to get back to Baker Street to attend to other matters of importance.

He did not make the return journey in as good time as he had come down, but it was very close, and when he walked into the consulting room at Baker Street, he was not surprised to see Tinker sitting at the desk writing busily.

"Well, my lad, did you have a good flight up?" he asked, as he removed his motoring coat and cap.

Tinker sprang to he feet. "Yes, guv'nor," he replied. "But something has happened which will annoy you."

"What is it?" asked Blake sharply.

"A telegram has just come from one of the coastguardsmen whom you took to Marsey Island, saying the the biplane returned before the T.B.D. showed up, and that in the fight that followed they—the two coastguardsmen—were overpowered, and left bound and helpless in the bungalow."

CHAPTER 4   Telling of a Meeting of the Brotherhood of the Yellow Beetle

Blake reached out his hand for the telegram which Tinker held, and hurriedly read the message. Dropping it on the desk with an exclamation of annoyance, he began to pace up and down the room.

"If I had only returned to Marsey Island," he muttered, "this would not have happened. I know how cunning Wu Ling and Beauremon are, and if they have joined forces they will make an ugly pair to fight. But if we had been on the island we should have had a chance in a million of raking the pair of them in. It is too bad—too bad! I—Answer it, Tinker," This as the telephone on the desk jangled shrilly.

Tinker lifted the receiver, but had said only a few words when he looked towards Blake. "It is the Munitions Minister, guv'nor."

Blake strode across to the desk and took the receiver.

"Hello!" he said.

"Hello! Is that you, Blake?" came a voice which he recognised as that of the Munitions Minister.

"Yes!" replied Blake.

"I have called you up to tell you that those people have got away, Blake." went on the Minister. "It is too bad. I should not have persuaded you to return to London, but should have let you return to the island, as you wished. You knew their capabilities better than I. But it is no use crying over spilt milk. They have got away and have taken with them the two men you caught."

"I know," replied Blake. "A wire has just come in about it. It is unfortunate."

"Still, we must get them, Blake," continued the Minister. "I have just heard from Sir John. He has received a code message from the commander of the T.B.D., which arrived at the island just after the affair was over. He says that he continued on his course up the Bristol Channel, and that not far off Cardiff he came upon a wrecked biplane—a machine far larger than the ordinary. It is not a Government machine, and from the description which Sir John gave me I imagine it is the one of which you spoke.

"At first the commander of the T.B.D. thought there had been an accident, but on examining the wreckage he became of the opinion that it had been deliberately disabled. Therefore, we can only conclude that the occupants had a rendezvous with a boat of some sort, and were picked up by it. The point is, what has become of them? And it is all the more important that we should find out, for Sir John tells me that he has heard vague reports of renewed activity on the part of German agents in England.

"It has occurred to me that these people who gave me their attention might be connected with this new German attempt. What do you think?"

"I think it is more than likely, sir," replied Blake. "When I say they are both capable of anything, I am not exaggerating. It is most unfortunate that they have escaped."

"That is exactly what I think, Blake. And I am glad you agree with me, for I want you take up the matter and run them to earth. Will you do so?"

Blake was silent for a few seconds. Not that he would refuse a definite request to handle a case for the Government, but because he knew it would take longer to run Wu Ling and Beauremon to earth a second time, and already his hands were full of urgent matters. However, he decided that other things must wait for the present, and so he replied:

"Certainly I will take it up, sir. Did Sir John have no further clue whatsoever as to what direction may have been taken by the occupants of the wrecked biplane?"

"I am afraid there is little to go upon," responded the Minister. "He did say that the commander of the T.B.D. had interviewed a fishing boat out of Bideford, and the crew of the smack told him they thought—only thought, mind you—that they had seen a motor boat in the vicinity of the wreckage. This may or may not be so, but it is the only thing in the shape of a clue. The fishermen said this motor boat went off at a high speed in the direction of Cardiff."

Blake pondered this bit of information for a moment, then said:

"Very well, sir, I shall go to work on the matter at once and see what I can discover. I shall make a report to you as soon as I know anything definite."

"Thank you, Blake!" rejoined the Minister. "I shall be greatly obliged to you."

With that he rang off, and Blake, rehanging the receiver, turned to Tinker.

"We shall have to leave London again, my lad. The Government thinks Wu Ling and Beauremon may be connected with some new activity on the part of the Germans, and want them run to earth. We must try to do so. Pack up the bags with some fresh things and see that the car is ready for a run to Cardiff. We shall start our search there, since that seems to be the only spot towards which even the vaguest of clues point. In the meantime, I shall get to work on this pile of letters and attend to anything urgent."

Tinker sprang up at once to obey, and hurried out to see to the preparations while Blake sat down at the desk and took up the huge pile of letters which lay on the blotting-pad. An hour later Blake has completed his task, and when Tinker appeared, carrying two large kit bags, he rose.

Donning their coats and caps, they once more entered the car, and taking the wheel, Blake turned and drove down Baker Street at a smart pace. It was a long and, after the journey they had both just completed, a particularly tiring ride down to Cardiff, and when they finally drew up in front of the Western Hotel, the major part of the inhabitants of the channel port were wrapped in slumber.

Rousing the night porter of the hotel they procured rooms, and when Tinker had driven the car into the hotel garage, they ascended at once to their apartments, knowing nothing could be done that night.

And yet, at the very moment when Blake and Tinker were in the act of retiring, there was a conference afoot in that same town of Cardiff, which, though it was held in secret, was proof sufficient that not all the town was sleeping.

In a house set in a narrow, dingy street, which led off the water front, there was a meeting in progress which, had Blake but known it, was to have a radical effect upon his own immediate fortunes.

In this darkened house, from which not a single chink of light was permitted to escape, there was a room which, like many rooms throughout the world, had been hung with heavy saffron-coloured silken curtains. There were no chairs or tables in the room, but round the sides had been piled great heaps of silken cushions—the prevailing tone of which was the all-pervading yellow.

The floor had been covered by a thick rug of intricate eastern pattern, the colours of which blended harmoniously with the cushions and hangings. From the ceiling hung a huge lamp wrought in copper, and in design not unlike an old Moorish brazier, although a connoisseur would have known that it was of an early Chinese period.

At the upper end of the apartment there had been placed a small dais, upon which had been piled a number of rich-looking cushions, and in front of the dais, within easy reach of it, was a tiny tabourette, upon which rested writing materials. It was a room of the Brotherhood of the Yellow Beetle, and on this night the council of the brotherhood was in session. On the cushions piled upon the dais sat Prince Wu Ling, of Manchu blood, royal legitimate heir to the ancient throne of China, authorised wearer of the sacred yellow and supreme head of that powerful organisation, the Brotherhood of the Yellow Beetle.

On this occasion he was garbed in the garments of his position— loose silken trousers of yellow, and a magnificent saffron-coloured tunic of heavy silk, caught together with a single great yellow topaz. On the breast of his coat glittered a single jewelled order, and one ring only—a massive affair set with a topaz—graced his hands.

He had changed little since his first entry into Europe in his great fight to place the heel of the yellow man on the neck of the white, and since that time in the far-off island of Kaitu, in the China Sea, when Sexton Blake had sent him perilously close to death.

His face was as inscrutably reposeful as ever—the same noble sweep to the brow was there—the hair was perhaps a little thinner, but still black as night, the deep-set oblique eyes, yet slumbrous and reflecting the lore of the ages gone. It was a face which reflected the power of the mind behind those who could see and read.

On this night he was bending forward where he sat, apparently in deep thought, and the members of the council of the brotherhood who were ranged down each side of the room were mutely patient, awaiting the pleasure of their lord.

Ten there were in all—ten sons of the East, who had been gathered from the ranks of the brotherhood and admitted to the sacred inner councils only after Wu Ling himself had tested them by the fire of the inquisition which he knew so well how to apply.

Not all the council of the Brotherhood was present. In Canton or Peking, when a full meeting was held, twenty-four attended, and on those occasions the conferences were affairs glittering with magnificence and lengthened by ceremony after ceremony, for there Wu Ling permitted himself the full sway of his power. But in London or New York, or elsewhere, when a meeting of the brotherhood was usually called to settle some policy of urgency, it was only attended, as on this occasion, by the members of the council who formed part of his personal suite. Yet, even then, the royal saffron was always in evidence.

For the better part of an hour Wu Ling had sat bent forward in thought, but as there was slight rustling sound at the far end of the room and the curtains swayed gently as a Celestial pushed them aside and entered, he raised his head and regarded the newcomer.

It was San, but a different San than usually attended upon his master. To-night his thick throat was swathed in white bandages, and he held his head at an angle as though in constant pain. And he was, for the bullet from Sexton Blake's rifle had been no flesh wound, but, as Blake himself had thought, had ploughed deep in the flesh of the Celestial's thick throat.

Then Wu Ling did a thing which, in all their experience of him, the members of the brotherhood had never seen him do. He rose, and treading with slow dignity, walked down the room to meet San.

As he did so the ten members rose as one man and stood with bent head while Wu Ling took San by the hand and led him back to the dais. There, on his own pile of cushions, he placed his wounded lieutenant, and, turning back to the others, bade them curtly to be seated.

When they were once more squatting on their piles of cushions, Wu Ling thrust his hands inside his tunic and began to address them.

"Members of the Brotherhood of the Yellow Beetle," he said in slow, guttural tones, "you have been summoned to-night to decide matters of urgency. I have waited until San—San, my faithful lieutenant, my tutor when I was but a youth, my substitute when you thought me dead, but when I was in reality in retreat in a Thibetan monastery—could attend before discussing the matters which must be discussed to-night. Before I do so, cast your eyes at San. The bandages which he wears speak for themselves.

"In all our dealing with the cursed white pigs, we have never suffered a greater set-back than we have this day. And members of the sacred brotherhood, it was due to one man who has been our Nemesis during the past, it is due to the man whose fingers were buried in my own throat on the Island of Kaitu, and who nearly succeeded in sending me to the arms of the blessed Confucius—to Sexton Blake—and may the god Mo send him to eternal perdition. And I, Wu Ling, tell you this night that this man must die.

"Listen, members of the Brotherhood of the Yellow Beetle, while I relate to you what has happened.

"At the last meeting of the Council of the Brotherhood, held in this same room, I told you of the arrangement which I had come to with the Germans. To us the German pigs are no more than the British pigs—may the god Mo take them all!—but in the furtherance of our great policy of world empire, in the crushing of the whites and in the placing of the saffron banner over all, it is necessary that we should play off the one against the other.

"For that reason I formed a temporary alliance with the Germans. I promised to lend them our aid in certain things, in return for which they were to give us a free hand in the East. We know how Japan has gone hand-in-hand with the British, and how they have forsaken the call of the East for the lure or the West. But we—we Chinese of the old empire, and the members of the Brotherhood of the Yellow Beetle, will keep the one goal in front of us and strive to reach it with the blessing of Confucius and Buddha—with the aid of the god Mo.

"In fulfilment of our agreement with the Germans, I went to see their prince when he came to England. As you know, our work then ended in failure, due, as in the past, to this dog Sexton Blake. Again, the Germans outlined a plan whereby the man who calls himself the British Minister of Munitions was to be taken and killed.

"On this man depend the present hopes of the British. He it is who holds in his hands the control of Britain and the output of munitions, which is her only hope at present. With him out of the way the Germans would achieve much in a single stroke.

"In order that there might be no miscarriage of plans, I enlisted the aid of a man whose deeds you have all heard of. He is a white man, but a man of decision and resource. I speak of Baron Robert de Beauremon, the head of an organisation known as the Council of Eleven. He accepted the offer I made him, and we set about to get possession of the person of this Minister of whom I have spoken. We succeeded and took him to a safe place of hiding where he was to be despatched.

"Realising how risky such a proceeding would be, we came to Cardiff in the big aeroplane, which is the property of the baron, in order to make arrangements for our escape after the Minister and his friend, whom we had captured with him, had been disposed of. While we were away San—San, my faithful lieutenant, whom you see wounded before you, was attacked, and he and Gonzalez, a Spaniard lieutenant of the baron's, were overpowered, while the prisoners we had taken were released.

"Only our opportune arrival enabled us to release San and the Spaniard before a British boat arrived to take them on board. And, members of the Council of the Brotherhood of the Yellow Beetle, the man who attacked San and released the two prisoners we had taken was this same man Sexton Blake. Therefore, I say to you, this man must die.

"More than once in the past has he been condemned to death, more than once has he been in our power, yet have the fates been with him. He has escaped, and still lives to oppose the will of the brotherhood. But this time he dies. I, Wu Ling, say it, and woe be to him who gets him into his power and allows him to escape. Yet I it must be to visit the death-stroke upon him. See that you do not forget that.

"Let the word go forth through all the Chinese in Cardiff, to all the Celestials, and members of the Brotherhood of the Yellow Beetle in England, that this man Blake must be taken. Not until he is removed from our path may we work successfully.

"Go forth, each one of you, this night, and spread the will of Wu Ling. I, Wu Ling, have spoken."

With that the prince sat down beside San, and for the space of five minutes or more, there was dead silence in the room. Then, slowly and almost noiselessly, the members of the council rose, and after bowing low before Wu Ling retired from the room.

When only Wu Ling and San were left, the prince once more rose, and walking to one corner of the apartment, drew aside the yellow curtains from a small stand which they had concealed. On this stand, which it might have been seen was of black marble, there reposed a small statue of a squatting god. It was of pure gold, which gleamed dully beneath the rays of the great central lamp, and sat upon a base of solid jade.

It was the god Mo, the patron god of Wu Ling—the image which watched over his destinies.

There, before the jade-based idol, he dropped to his knees and bent in submission until his forehead touched the floor.

For some minutes he remained thus, then rose to his feet and made a gesture for San to follow him from the room.

He had prayed to the golden god Mo to favour his vendetta against Sexton Blake, and he was certain in his own mind that the god would hear him.

The morning following their arrival in Cardiff, Blake and Tinker were abroad early. Blake's decision to start investigations at Cardiff was simply the result of a direct assumption that the wrecked biplane, which had been found floating in the Bristol Channel, was the one which had been used in the kidnapping of the Munitions Minister and his friend, Sir Hector Amworth.

If it should prove to be another machine, then he would have to pick up some other line of suggestion. But so far, he was strongly of the opinion that the wreckage was that of the big biplane belonging to the Council of Eleven.

Ever since he had been called down to Westward Ho! in order to trace the Munitions Minister, Cardiff had been more or less connected with the affair.

For instance, it will be recalled that when Tinker was flying from Hendon to Westward Ho! and had seen another machine over the Bristol Channel, he had been of the opinion that it had come from Cardiff way.

Then again, the fact that it was able to visit Marsey Island so frequently, and at such short intervals, proved that it had a base not very far distant—that is, not far distant when considering the radius of action of an aeroplane.

Furthermore, the message which had come through from the commander of the T.B.D. had said that the wreckage had been found in the Bristol Channel, not far from Cardiff, and that the fishermen whom he had interviewed had spoken of a motor-boat which they had seen in the vicinity of the wreckage, and which they thought had made off towards Cardiff.

So Blake's quick decision to go to Cardiff and open the new investigation there was not the result of any lengthy deduction, but simply the result of the rapidity with which long experience had enabled him to put his finger on the most likely spot in a case.

He knew, too, that Cardiff possessed a very large Chinese element, and since Prince Wu Ling had climbed into the realm of European diplomatic scheming, Cardiff had more than once been the base of his British operations.

Blake was dead certain in his own mind that Wu Ling had played a leading part in the daring outrage on the Munitions Minister and Sir

Hector Amworth. That Baron Robert de Beauremon was also mixed up in the affair he felt confident, but he knew when he found one he would find the other.

The difficulty was to locate them before they shifted their base from Cardiff. They would realise how dangerous that locality would be for them after the rescue of the Munitions Minister, and would use every despatch to make a shift in base.

Therefore, speed was essential if Blake were to track them down before they moved and thus complicated matters. But first he wished to prove one point. He wished to get into touch with the commander of the T.B.D., and to get from that gentleman a detailed description of the wreckage which he had come upon. He wished, also, to find the two coastguards who had been overpowered on Marsey Island, and to receive from them a description of the men who had come to the island. That would take time, but it must be done.

From the Munitions Minister he knew that Cardiff was the base of the T.B.D., and that being so he would have little difficulty in finding the commander. But to speak with the coastguards he must have them across from Westward Ho!

His first duty in the morning, after sending Tinker on a scouting expedition along the water front, was to hire a motorboat and send it across the channel to Westward Ho! to get the two coastguards. Then he set about to look for the T.B.D.

After a couple of hours about the water front he heard from a certain source that she would be in harbour about noon, so he loitered about until that hour watching for her.

Sure enough midday had just gone when her black nose poked its way into port, and scarcely was she moored when Blake was aboard her.

When the commander was made aware of Blake's identity he invited him down into his cabin, and there, in answer to the detective's questions, gave him a detailed description of the wreckage which he had come upon, and after taking note of, had sunk to prevent it from being a menace to navigation.

From the notes which he had taken Blake got sufficient information to convince him that it was none other than the big biplane used by the Council of Eleven, and when he had thanked the commander for his help took his leave.

He walked back towards the Western Hotel, and just as he

reached the portals of that caravanserai met Tinker, who was obviously in a state of excitement.

"I have something important to tell you, guv'nor," he whispered, as they entered the lobby.

Blake nodded slightly.

"Come upstairs at once, Tinker," he replied, scarcely moving his lips.

They ascended in the lift, and walked along the corridor to their sitting-room. There Blake closed and locked the door, and, after a careful search round the room, signed to Tinker.

"Now, go ahead, my lad," he said.

Tinker stood close to his master, and speaking in a low tone said:

"I saw San in Cardiff this morning, guv'nor."

Blake glanced at the lad sharply.

"Are you certain?" he asked quickly.

"Dead certain, guv'nor," responded Tinker, "when I left here to scout about, I made for the docks. I saw you more than once during the morning, but I kept out of sight. I went up in the Chinese part—you remember where we had a mix-up when we were on that Sacred Sphere[3] business?—and scouted about there with some of the crews who were knocking round from pub to pub.

"Well, I had been in half a dozen or more—they took me for a ship's boy—when just as we were leaving one to go to another, the door of a house opened and a Chinaman came out. His neck and the side of face were all in bandages, but I recognised him in a moment as San. I slipped away from the gang a few minutes later and shadowed him. He walked down to the docks and idled about for a little, then he returned to the house from which I had seen him come out.

"He looked pretty bad, guv'nor, and I guess he was only out for a constitutional. Anyway, he disappeared back into the house, and I came straight on here to report.

"Which house do you refer to, Tinker?" asked Blake curtly.

"I mean the one, guv'nor, which you said was an opium joint."

Blake gazed at the carpet thoughtfully.

"I remember the place," he muttered to himself—"a long, low building, with the shutters always closed. It poses as a lodging-house, and in one corner there is a pub. Is that the one?"

---

[3] Stillwoods publication--- http://www.lulu.com/shop/g-h-teed/the-sacred-sphere/paperback/product-23958942.html

"That's it, guv'nor."

"And San is there," went on Blake. "If he is there, it means Wu Ling is not far away. I thought we should strike their trail in Cardiff, and it seems you have done so, my lad. But we must lose no time in getting after them. San is important, but can wait. It is Wu Ling himself we must gather in. This needs some thought, Tinker."

Walking to the window, Blake stood for a long time gazing out at the street below. Tinker, knowing that Blake was revolving in his mind some plan to gain access to the Chinese joint and to follow up the clue he had found, sat down and waited patiently for his master to decide the next step.

Finally Blake turned back from the window.

"Get out my Chinese disguise, my lad—not the mandarin one, but that of a coolie."

"Then you are going there, guv'nor?" asked Tinker.

Blake nodded.

"It is the only way."

"If they get you, guv'nor you will never get out alive!" said the lad earnestly. "You know how hot they are to rope you in after that last brush you had with Wu Ling. It is only a little time since they had us besieged in Baker Street and nearly got us both. If you are suspected in this Chinese joint it will be 'Good-night, nurse' with you pretty quick!"

Blake shrugged his shoulders.

"I am not anxious to go into the place, my lad. I realise as well as you how keen the Brotherhood of the Yellow Beetle is to 'get me,' but I can see no other way. Wu Ling and his crowd are getting altogether too daring in England! They must be stopped, and stopped at once! It was bad enough when they were fighting only for themselves, but now that they have joined up with the Germans, as we know they have, something must be done to clean them out of the place.

"Therefore I shall go to this house. But I shall take all necessary precautions, never fear, and before I go will arrange as far as possible for my safety. There will be work for you to do outside while I am there. Now get my disguise out, and then we shall have some lunch before I change."

Without further protest, Tinker rose, though he did not like Blake's plan. But he knew if his master thought the only thing to do was to enter the camp of the enemy, he would do that thing regardless of the danger it held for him. Nor had the lad forgotten some of his own experiences while in the hands of Wu Ling and his men.

When he had got out the disguise, Tinker returned to the sitting-room and joined Blake. Together they descended to the dining-room, where they ate a hurried lunch. After lunch they went up again to the sitting-room of their suite, and when he had smoked a cigarette Blake prepared to make the change in appearance from that of a keen-looking Londoner to that of a Chinese coolie.

Going into his bedroom, he sat down before the dressing-table and, drawing towards him a large black box of pigments, set to work first on his face.

With a yellowish stain, which he had procured from the Celebes, in the Dutch East Indies, he stained all the skin of the face, neck, and arms. When this had dried, he took up a pencil affair with which he drew hundreds of tiny almost invisible lines, which, although not visible at any great distance, still gave that lined and seamed appearance so typical in the Chinese countenance.

That done, he set to work on his eyebrows, which he blackened carefully. Then he gave his attention to the eyes themselves, working away at them until they presented the oblique appearance of the ordinary Celestial.

Not until he was quite satisfied with this did he pick up the black queued wig which was a tonsorial masterpiece of one of the cleverest West End hairdressers.

Adjusting it carefully, Blake next turned to the garments. On his legs he drew loose trousers of cheap blue cotton, then slipped his feet into the thick-soled slippers so favoured of the coolie. Next he drew on a loose coat which buttoned well up, and, that done, he regarded himself at length in the glass.

He was dissatisfied with one or two points of detail, and proceeded to change them, after which he walked out to the sitting-room where Tinker waited.

The lad rose and cast a critical eye at his master. Over every detail that sharp young gaze went until it had covered Blake from head to foot. Then he nodded.

"It will do, guv'nor. I can't see a single fault."

Blake smiled.

"Then I shall prepare to go along, my lad," he said. "I think you had better accompany me out of the hotel. I don't want to arouse any comment, which might be the case should I go out alone. But before I go I shall post you in what you have to do. Now listen carefully!

"This afternoon you will hang about the docks, and keep an eye out for the arrival of the motorboat which I sent across to Westward Ho! to get the two coastguards. When you have seen them, you will get from them a description of the men who landed on Marsey Island and overpowered them. Get them to sign it. We shall need it in the evidence we shall bring against Wu Ling and Beauremon.

"When you have done that, give them a couple of sovereigns each, and see that they get away again for Westward Ho! If any of Wu Ling's crowd should get on to the fact that they are here, it might go badly with them. The next thing you will do is to go to the police. See the chief of police of the city, and make yourself known to him. Then tell him exactly why we are down here and what we propose doing. Enlist his aid. He will be glad to do all he can to assist you. Have him get a half a dozen men together. I would suggest that they be either plain-clothes men or special constables. If the latter, they can remove their badges, and then there will be little about them to arouse suspicion.

"This force you will hold in readiness until midnight to-night. If by then I have not returned to the Western Hotel, you will know that trouble has arisen, and will start at once for the house to which I am going. There you will raid it, and search it from top to bottom.

"Do not miss a single corner of it! You know as well as I do how cunning the Chinese are in the locating of secret rooms which they do not wish the police to find. Raze the place if necessary, but do not desist from your search until you have found me, because, if I have not returned from there by midnight, it will only be because I have found it impossible to do so. Do you understand exactly what you have to do?"

"Perfectly, guv'nor," replied Tinker, with a worried frown. "But, all the same, I don't like it! I wish you would let me go down there and hang about! These Chinks are out after your blood, and if they dream for a single moment that you are not what you appear to be, they will not rest until they have discovered your identity. Then— well, you know what will happen to you!"

Blake shrugged.

"It can't be helped, my lad. I am going after Wu Ling and

72

Beauremon, and it is the only way I can get on their trail. Do what I have told you, and we will trust to luck and my ingenuity. Come!"

Blake turned as he spoke and, on opening the door, passed out into the corridor, followed by Tinker. Passing along, they avoided the lift and descended by the staircase in order not to arouse too much comment.

Arriving in the lobby, they hastened out on to the street almost before the few persons who loitered there were aware that a Celestial had just gone past. Then, when they were a hundred yards or so down the street, Tinker, with a whispered word to his master, slipped away, and Blake went on alone to enter the den of the Yellow Tiger of the East.

Nor, as he did so, did he dream for a single moment that as they had emerged from the Western Hotel a sleek-looking Chinaman in a shop across the street had seen them come out, and, remembering the order of Wu Ling which had swept through the Chinese element that very morning, and consequently suspicious at seeing a coolie emerge from the hotel in the company of a white lad, had slipped forth from the shop to follow him.

Down the street he went, his slant-eyes half closed, and apparently seeing nothing of his surroundings. Yet from beneath those heavy lids he was watching every step of the two ahead, and then Tinker left Blake, the Celestial trailed the coolie.

On and on went Blake, all unsuspicious of the man who followed him, and away towards the docks went Tinker, equally unsuspicious.

This was by no means the first time Sexton Blake had played the part of a Celestial. Often in the past had it been necessary for him to adopt the role, and, with a perfect command of the different spoken dialects of China, as well as a deep knowledge of the written language of that country, he had carried out the daring project with brilliant success.

Take Sexton Blake, garb him as a Celestial, and drop him into the centre of Canton, and if the Chinese of that ancient city did not know that he was not one of them, they would never find out the truth through any defect in Blake's appearance or slip in his speech.

He had even spoken with Wu Ling as Celestial to Celestial, and the prince had not suspected his identity, and the man who could fool Wu Ling could fool all China.

Arriving at the corner of the street in which was situated the house of which Tinker had spoken, Blake paused for a moment, and gazed sleepily about him, as any other Celestial might have done. Then, turning, he shuffled along the street until he came to the house which was his objective.

Arriving at it, he did not make any attempt to enter it by means of the door, which was apparently for the use of the regular occupants, but, instead, he passed into the saloon part of the place. There, in front of the bar, he saw half a dozen Celestials and seaman of sorts drinking and tossing dice.

Slouching up to the bar, Blake ordered a drink from the Chinaman who was serving, and, with that before him, leaned idly against the bar.

He had not been standing there long when one of the Celestials who had been shaking dice sidled up to him.

"You are a stranger?" he said in low, guttural Chinese.

Blake turned his sleepy eyes upon the other.

"I have come from London," he said.

For a moment the other regarded him impassively, then, bending forward towards the bar, he said, scarcely moving his lips:

"Are you of the East?"

Blake's heart leaped, though his features were as inscrutable as those of the other. The words he had just heard formed the opening phrase of the test of membership of the Brotherhood of the Yellow Beetle, and only too well he remembered the stinking river den in Canton where he had first heard them, and from the memories of the past there came to him the answer.

"Of the East and for the East," he replied slowly.

"Where do you go?" came the next question.

"Into the West," answered Blake readily.

"Do you return?" asked his interlocutor.

"There is no return," responded Blake. "The West will be East."

With that the Celestial sidled still closer, confident from Blake's reply that he was a member of the Brotherhood.

"You will stay in Cardiff long?" he asked.

Blake shrugged, and drew out some yellow cigarette-paper, into which he poured some tobacco.

"Who knows?" he said, as he rolled a cigarette. "Perhaps a day, perhaps a year. It is the will of Buddha. Will the honourable one drink with one so unworthy?"

The Celestial nodded.

"If you will permit one so unworthy to drink in your presence," he replied.

Blake made a sign to the man behind the bar, who filled up two fresh glasses, and pushed them across.

Then Blake and the Celestial pledged each other with the flowery and meaningless compliments of the East.

When they set down their glasses again the Celestial glanced at Blake.

"Do you come in ignorance?" he asked.

Blake puffed slowly at his cigarette.

"I know nothing," he replied.

"The Illustrious One is in Cardiff!" went on the Chinaman, in a low tone.

Blake bowed his head reverently.

"My vile ears are unworthy to hear such news?" he said. "Is the great Illustrious One indeed here?"

"He is here, and has made known his will," responded the Celestial. "He does much for the good of the Brotherhood. The Yellow Dragon will yet wave over this country of pigs. The Illustrious One has spoken."

Blake smoked on, waiting for the other to continue. It was evident to him from what he had just heard that Wu Ling was undoubtedly in Cardiff, and that something special was afoot.

Even the stolid Celestial beside him was affected by the importance of it. And he knew by waiting he would hear what it was.

"The order has gone forth," went on the other, after a little. "There is one whom it is the will of the Illustrious One to find, and when he has found him—" And he finished with a shrug. "There is one who is a white pig. He has done much to annoy the Illustrious One, and the Brotherhood is to take revenge for the daring of the contemptible pig. His name is Blake—Sexton Blake—and the Illustrious One has deigned to command that every member of the sacred Brotherhood shall seek him out, and bring him to the seat of judgment. All the members in this cursed country know the will of the Illustrious One."

Blake nodded slowly.

"And this pig, Blake," he said—"what is he like?"

The Celestial beside him laid one hand on the bar.

"He is tall as the sapling in the forest," he said. "He is strong as the oak which bends, but breaks not, beneath the blast. He is neither young nor old. He is cunning—ah, so cunning! Not even in the East are there any more cunning than he. I have heard that in the past he has dared more than once to oppose the will of the Illustrious One. Do you remember when the Illustrious One was not with us for a time?"

"Do I remember that the sun was out?" replied Blake, meaning that the great orb of day had not shone while Wu Ling was absent.

"It was this same pig, Blake, who nearly sent the Illustrious One to the arms of the blessed Confucius," went on the Celestial, referring to the time in the island of Kaitu when Blake had choked Wu Ling into insensibility, and had nearly sent the prince to his death. "The Illustrious One is sending out a picture of the pig, so that all shall know him and watch for him."

Blake nodded again.

"It is well," he responded. "The pig, Blake, will be sought on all sides by the Brotherhood. May I be the one to find him!"

The Celestial bowed in agreement, then said:

"Have you been in the opium-room yet?"

Blake made a gesture of negation.

"No," he replied. "I have but come. I go to seek it now."

"I know it well," went on his companion. "I will take you to it for the price of two pills."

"I will give you the price of one," rejoined Blake, not forgetting to bicker as any other Celestial would have done.

"It is well," said the other. "Come!"

Blake, well pleased at the prospect of gaining admittance to the opium-room under the wing of a regular habitue, turned and followed. His guide kicked open a low door leading into the next room where Blake saw a few Chinamen gaming after the stolid manner of their kind.

Past these, who never once glanced in their direction, they went until they reached a door on the opposite side of the room. Opening this they passed into another corridor.

Like a giant Chinese puzzle-box was that den. Leaving the corridor into which they had just come, they passed through room after room, his guide going ahead with the confidence of one perfectly familiar with his surroundings, and as one who was persona grata in the place. And the nearer they approached to the heart of the place the more mysterious became the subtle air of something concealed which pervaded it.

Here and there in small shadowy rooms sat little groups of Celestials, talking in low tones, and planning Heaven only knew what schemes. In others, too gloomy to be pierced by the eye, Blake could feel the presence of people, whose occupation might almost be anything which skulked under the wing of darkness.

On and on still further through the puzzle-box Blake went, glimpsing scenes which could not be described, and which, if they were, would scarcely be believed, and then at last his guide brought him to the opium-room, where on long mattresses, piled close together, lay the victims of the drug, lying in every attitude of repulsive abandon, saturated with opium the drug which, as long as it is submerged beneath its thrall, will prevent the Chinese nation from being really great.

There, from out of the shadows a Celestial shuffled up, and with him Blake's guide held a whispered colloquy. Finally, he turned to Blake.

"It is well," he said, in a whisper. "Give me the price of the two pills which you promised."

Blake, who knew the scale of prices in half the opium-dens in the world, held out the price of one shot, and the other, seeing that he would gain nothing by haggling, seized it, and shuffled towards a mattress.

Blake, in reply to an inquiry from the pipe attendant, expressed his wish to smoke, and the latter conducted him to a mattress at the other end of the room. There Blake cast himself down, and while he was waiting for the attendant to prepare his pipe, and to arrange the tiny pill of opium, he gazed about him.

Nearly all the mattresses were occupied, though it was still early in the day. Some were already in the throes of the drug-dreams, muttering and mumbling incoherently, proving that they had been there for some time, possibly since the day before. Others were less advanced in the grip of the drug, and still more were but preparing to take their first shot.

The atmosphere of the place was heavy and fetid, with a nauseating suggestion which affected even Blake, accustomed though he was to such places. Probably not for years had the light of day been permitted to enter the room. What windows there were, were heavily shuttered, and inside those hung heavy curtains effectually cutting off all light.

The men on the mattresses were of all sorts and conditions, though Blake could not help but note that in this particular joint they were all Celestials.

When the attendant had affixed the tiny pill of opium to his pipe, Blake put the mouthpiece between his lips, and, settling himself down, prepared to smoke. He knew that he must take some of the drug in order to remain in the place without suspicion, but he had no intention of permitting himself to be overcome by it.

From what he had already discovered he knew that Wu Ling was either in the place at that very moment, or else very close to it. And it was to find Wu Ling he had come there.

But clever though his disguise was, and perfect though his command of the language might be, they were to prove of little assistance to him as he was to find out, for the sleek-looking Celestial who had seen him leave the hotel with Tinker had not by any means had his suspicions allayed.

Even while Blake had stood by the bar talking with the other Chinaman, had he stood outside, peering in idly from time to time, and watching every movement of the man who had aroused his suspicions. Then, when Blake had disappeared from the bar, and had entered the joint proper, he had slipped into the bar, and, standing close to it, had asked the man who was serving what he knew about the Celestial who had just drunk there.

When he was told that Blake was a total stranger to the place, and that by his own words he had but arrived from London, the sleek-looking one had grown more suspicious than ever, and, in his sleepy Chinese fashion, had pondered deeply.

At the end of some ten minutes or so when, as it happened, the bar held very few people, he leaned across to the man who was serving, and, in low, guttural tones, said:

"Is the Illustrious One within?"

The other gazed at him impassively for a few moments before replying.

"Son and grandson of pigs that thou art, why do you speak of the Illustrious One?"

"The open mouth catches the flies," responded Number One slowly. "I have word for the ear of the Illustrious One. Go and beg that he will permit the sun of his countenance to shine upon me."

The serving man bent his head a little lower.

"If you seek to waste the time of the Illustrious One, you will be as the blade before the blast, and will wither before the scorn of his august eye."

"I seek not the presence of the Illustrious One without wheat to bring him," replied Number One. "Go and seek him."

The man behind the bar turned, and, shuffling along, lifted up a dirty curtain which shut off the bar from the room beyond. He passed through and dropped it behind him, and for the space of ten minutes or so the man who stood by the bar waited.

Then the curtain was once more lifted, and the bar-tender reappeared.

Lifting a finger he beckoned to the other, and he, with a slight motion of the hand, walked along to a flap in the counter. Lifting this he passed behind the bar, and joined the bar-tender.

Through a small room the latter led him, and then along a narrow passage lit by a single light. At the end of this passage the guide stopped and knocked thrice. A guttural voice on the other side of the door bade him enter, and, opening the door, he passed through, followed by the other.

The room into which they passed was a small apartment, furnished only with a table and a rough chair. In this chair, writing, sat a Celestial who looked up as the two entered. The bar-tender stepped forward.

"I have brought the presumptuous pig," he said.

The Chinaman at the table regarded the one referred to.

"Why do you seek the Illustrious One?" he asked curtly.

The Celestial, who had followed Blake so closely, spread out his hands.

"I have important word for the ear of the master," he said slowly. "I would speak with him at once. It is about the order which the Illustrious One has sent out to all members of the Brotherhood."

The heavy lids of the man at the table dropped a little lower.

"If you have news, the Illustrious One will be pleased to admit you to his honourable presence, but if you talk as the cuckoo, woe betide you!"

"I have news," replied the other simply.

The man at the table rose, and made a motion to the bar-tender, which caused him to leave the room. Then the former approached a door in the opposite wall, and beckoned to the other.

"Come!" he said. "I will take you to the Illustrious One."

Through a maze of passages and small rooms he now led the newsbringer until at last he stopped before a door, which was almost hidden from view by heavy curtains. Pushing them aside the guide knocked, and a moment later, in answer to a summons from within, opened the door and entered.

The moment he was inside the door he bowed low, and stood waiting until ordered to advance. Then he lifted his head and went forward. The room was the same wherein there had been held a meeting of the Brotherhood the previous evening.

On the cushions before the dais at the upper end sat Wu Ling and beside him, with his throat still swathed in bandages, was San. There was no one else in the room.

"There is one who would speak to you, Illustrious One," said the guide.

Wu Ling, still clad in the saffron tunic of the Brotherhood, made a gesture.

"Let him approach," he said curtly.

The guide again bowed, and, backing out, took the news-bringer by the sleeve.

"Go in," he whispered, "and see that you trifle not with the Illustrious One."

The other nodded, and, pushing between the curtains, stepped into the room. He stood for a full minute with bent head while Wu Ling's all-seeing gaze swept him from head to foot. Finally the prince spoke:

"You are of the Brotherhood?" he asked curtly.

"Oh, Illustrious One, I have been of it long,"

"You bring important word?" went on Wu Ling. "Have you thought well before seeking my presence?"

"Oh Illustrious One," replied the news-bringer, "I sought the sun of your presence because I have word of importance. It is to speak of the Illustrious One's order that I come."

Wu Ling lifted his head a trifle.

"Advance and speak!" he ordered.

The Chinaman walked up the room, until he stood nearer the dais, then he said:

"Oh, Illustrious One, your order went abroad this morning, and we of the Brotherhood hearkened and were glad. It was only when I had heard that I was standing in the shop of Looey Wan Kai. As I talked with the unworthy pig, Illustrious One, I saw two who came forth from the hotel of the white pigs, which is just across the street.

"One, Illustrious One, was a Celestial, but the other was a young white pig. It seemed strange to me, Illustrious One, that one of the East should come forth from the place with a white pig, and, Illustrious One, he was not dressed as one of the elect, but as a coolie.

"I followed them along until the young white pig took leave of the Celestial; then I followed the son of the East. He came even to this place, Illustrious One, and after drinking at the bar with Fan Hei, whom I recognised, they passed into the opium room. Then, Illustrious One, did I enter the bar and make question.

"He who served behind the bar told me that the man whom I followed was a stranger to him, and that he had heard him tell Fan Hei he was but arrived from London. It was strange that he should issue forth from the hotel of the white pigs, Illustrious One. With the order of the Brotherhood in my mind, I pondered, Illustrious One. He may be a traitor, else why should he, a coolie, be with the white pigs? Even now he is in the opium-room. That is the word I would bring you."

As he finished speaking, he again bowed he head submissively, waiting for Wu Ling to speak.

At last the prince did so. "If your word is true, if, with the eye of the eagle, you have seen the gliding snake, then shall your reward be great indeed. You say this dog of a coolie is even now within the place?"

"He is in the opium-room, Illustrious One. Also Fan Hei watches that he passes not out without being followed."

"That is well," said Wu Ling. "I shall see to this dog."

Then he turned to San.

"San," he ordered, "go to the opium-room and have speech with the attendant. See that no one leaves it or enters until he have had our will."

San rose at once, and bowing low, shuffled from the room.

When the curtains had dropped after him Wu Ling rose and made a gesture for the news-bringer to follow him. Lifting up the curtains at one side of the room, Wu Ling pressed a part of the wall, and immediately a wide low panel slid back noiselessly.

Stepping through into a dark passage beyond, he waited for the other to follow him. Then, closing the panel, he walked with slow dignity down the full length of the passage until he came to a door at the end. Opening this he entered a small room, and crossing to the opposite wall, released a panel there.

When they had passed through, the news-bringer saw that they were standing in a tiny apartment completely hung with curtains of heavy black velvet and illuminated by a small copper lamp which hung from the centre of the ceiling.

It was utterly devoid of furniture, and to the uninitiated, it's use would be a mystery. But San could have told that it was the room from which Wu Ling at times inspected the opium-room, and where he listened to the maudlin maunderings of the drug fiends.

More than once had the prince heard the secrets of a man's soul by listening there, and more than once had some poor creature gone forth from that opium-room to an unknown fate—a fate decreed by the prince as a penalty to the indiscreet.

There was never any mercy, any appeal in the Brotherhood of the Yellow Beetle. When a man was once sentenced to death, nothing could alter the decree.

Wu Ling stepped close to the black velvet curtains, and, pushing one of them aside, disclosed a small panel which was scarcely large enough to permit one to place both eyes before it.

Before pushing it back he beckoned to the other to step close, then gently he slid the bit of rosewood to one side. Bending towards it he peered through at the opium-room beyond, and slowly swept the apartment with his gaze. A gesture brought the news-bringer beside him, and Wu Ling pointed towards the panel.

"Look through and tell me which one is the traitor?" he whispered.

The other did as he was bid, and after peering through for a moment, raised his head.

"It is the dog on the third mattress from this end on the left, Illustrious One," he said.

Wu Ling again bent close, and for a long minute regarded the man who had been pointed out to him. Nor was he in danger of being seen by the coolie, who lay on the mattress sucking at the pipe, for the panel was cunningly concealed from view of anyone in the opium-room by a thin lattice-work screen, which, while it permitted one from the observation-room to see the whole of the opium apartment, still prevented any in that place from seeing the observer.

At last Wu Ling straightened up and softly closed the panel.

"I know not the coolie dog," he said slowly. "But we shall know more of him soon. Wait here until my order comes to you."

With that Wu Ling glided from the room, and the news-bringer squatted on the floor to wait.

On the mattress in the opium-room, sucking at his third pipe, lay Sexton Blake. Ever since the attendant had prepared his first pill had Blake lain there smoking and peering out from heavy-lidded eyes to see and to hear what he could.

From the broken snatches of maudlin ravings about him he had caught nothing of value, nor in the few new arrivals who had appeared did he see anything of interest. But still he remained there, determined to discover in some way if Wu Ling were really in the place.

As time went on and the life of the den revealed nothing. Blake began to ponder deeply, trying to devise some method for gaining access to even deeper and more secret parts of the joint—parts which he knew must exist.

Once he could run the gauntlet of the outer line of the place he knew that he would come upon things which stopped short at the opium-room.

Yet little did he dream that at that very moment Wu Ling himself was gazing at him through a tiny panel in one end of the room. Nor did he realise how dire was the peril in which he was.

Blake was still smoking his third pipe when the attendant shuffled past him to the upper end of the room. In the shadows here Blake could just see the blue jacket which he wore, and from the fellow's attitude Blake knew he was holding a conversation with some new arrival, though he could not see the person of the latter.

Then, for the barest fraction of a second, the new arrival stepped within Blake's line of vision, and he could have sworn that he had caught a glimpse of a head swathed in bandages. The head was withdrawn so quickly that he could not make sure, but with the suggestion came the thought of San, whom he himself had shot at Marsey Island. And with that same thought a great uneasiness filled Blake.

He lay back with closed eyes as the attendant shuffled back down the room, and could almost feel the gaze of the other upon him as he passed by. Then the footsteps came near again, and upon his ears broke the voice of the attendant.

"Will the honourable one smoke more?" he asked.

"One—one more pipe," he said in the thick voice of the smoker who is falling under the effects of the drug.

The attendant bowed, and, leaning over, laid his hand on the pipe. At the same moment Blake caught another glimpse of a swathed head at the upper end of the apartment, and once more the feeling of uneasiness swept over him.

Through him swept a wave of presentiment. Something within him rang out a clarion call of warning, and, regardless of everything, Blake started to rise, determined to get out of the place while he might.

Then, as he was still half sitting up, the attendant suddenly withdrew his hands from the pipe, and with a hissing sound pushed Blake back. Blake, realising now that for some reason suspicion against him had been aroused, started up again.

There was a sound behind him, and he turned to meet any attack which might come from that direction. But he was too late.

Even as he swung round, a panel in the wall behind him was pushed back, and from the darkness beyond there came a flying yellow cord, which looped and circled over his head, then fell to his shoulders.

A second later it was drawn tight about his throat, and as, choking and gasping, and with senses reeling, he struggled to free himself, Blake became aware that several yellow faces were bearing down upon him.

The Yellow Tiger had struck.

*　　*　　*　　*　　*

Once again the meeting of the council of the Brotherhood of the Yellow Beetle was in progress, but far, far different was the spirit which animated it from that of the former meeting which had been held in that same room only the evening before.

No smile lit up those impassive faces, nor was there any relaxation of dignified ceremony in their conduct of the meeting. But yet, from squatting Celestial to squatting Celestial there seemed to pass a feeling of anticipation which held them tense.

On his pile of cushions before the dais sat Wu Ling, with San beside him as usual. And once the members were assembled, Wu Ling wasted no time in getting to business. Rising, he held up his hand.

"Members of the Brotherhood of the Yellow Beetle," he said slowly, "you have been called into council to-night to consider important matters. Last night we met here and I made known my will regarding the white pig, Sexton Blake. This morning the order went out to the members of the Brotherhood throughout the world.

"This afternoon, a humble member of the Brotherhood, who had received word of my will, saw that which aroused his suspicions. From a hotel of the white pigs he saw two men issue—a young white dog and a Celestial. That hotel is the resort of the white pigs who have much wealth, and, members of the council, that Celestial was a coolie. It was not seemly that a coolie should issue forth from such a place in the company of a white pig.

"The faithful member of the Brotherhood followed them and soon the white pig went his way. The member continued on the heels of the coolie and followed him to this place—the headquarters of the Brotherhood in Cardiff. He came into this place and drank at the bar, then he went to the opium-room, where he smoked.

"To me the faithful one came with the word, and I myself looked in upon this coolie, whose actions were as the ways of the snake. Then I gave the order to gather him in and it was done. Before me was the coolie brought, and San saw to it that he was prepared for the inquiry. And, members of the council, when that was done, it was discovered that he was no coolie, but a white pig, and more, he was the white pig which it was the chief aim of the Brotherhood of the Yellow Beetle to find.

"The 'coolie' was Sexton Blake himself. How he managed to get in here you know. But the man himself shall be brought before you, and then the sentence of the Brotherhood shall be passed upon him."

There was a faint stir as Wu Ling finished speaking, but scarcely had his voice died away when the curtains at the far end of the room were pushed aside, and two Celestials entered, dragging a third man with them. Between the rows of squatting Chinese they passed, until they were in front of the dais, then at a gesture from Wu Ling, they stood aside from their prisoner.

And what a woeful-looking object he was. There he stood in the coarse garments of a coolie, but with the queued wig torn from his head, and the yellow pigment all blotchy and streaky.

Yet through it could be seen the clean-cut features and deep-set, grey eyes of Sexton Blake, who when the hands of his captors had dropped away drew himself up and gazed straight into Wu Ling's eyes.

Even had he dared try to escape it would have been useless, for his wrists were bound securely behind him, and about his ankles were two steel cuffs connected by a chain, which, while it gave sufficient freedom to the feet to permit him to shuffle along, forbade a stride of any length.

Wu Ling gave back gaze for gaze; then, raising his hand, spoke to the members of the Brotherhood.

"Behold the man," he said curtly. "Regard him well; you who have not seen him before. There stands the man who has set himself against the Brotherhood of the Yellow Beetle from its inception—the man who has tried time and again to drive us to ruin—the man whose hands sought to encompass my death in our own sacred island of Kaitu.

"He has been in my power more than once in the past, but Destiny was with him, and he escaped. But now he is mine again, and this time he shall meet the fate which is to be his. As well might he try to escape from the yellow dragon as to escape our clutches now. Members of the Brotherhood, he is here to hear your will. He who would speak let him do so."

All during the harangue Blake had stood with a contemptuous smile upon his lips—a smile which must have maddened Wu Ling to see, though the Celestial showed no sign that he noticed it.

When he had finished speaking a stout Celestial, who sat some distance down the line on the right-hand side, rose, and bowing low, said:

"Oh, Illustrious One, with your permission, my unworthy lips would frame a remark?"

Wu Ling inclined his head.

"Speak," he said.

The member stepped forward a little, and raising one hand, pointed full at Blake.

"He is the man, Illustrious One, who would have deprived us of the sun of your presence. Only one fate can be his—death. And it is meant that death should be the death of the Sacred Beetle. He sleeps within his cell, Illustrious One; he hungers for his pleasure, Illustrious One. Let him be brought forth and let him feed upon the throat of this white pig, even as the throat of His Excellency San was seared by the white pig's bullets."

The Chinaman bowed again and withdrew to his place. Then rose up member after member to put forth the same plea that Blake should be at once executed by the poisonous beetle from which the Brotherhood takes its name.

Wu Ling heard them all out, when the last had sat down he turned to San.

"And you San," he said, "what fate think you should be his?"

San rose slowly.

"It is the pleasure of the Illustrious One," he said. "What the Illustrious One says is my will."

Wu Ling then turned back to the members of the council.

"Members of the Brotherhood," he said, "I have heard you, and you speak well. But the death of the beetle is not to be the death of this white pig Blake. I have another fate in store for him. Hark you! To the god Mo I prayed that the dog Blake might be given into my hands. Lo! the god Mo heard me, and this very day delivered my enemy unto me.

"Therefore I, Wu Ling, say to you that his fate shall be this. To the island of Kaitu—the sacred isle in the China Sea—shall he be taken, and there shall he be offered up as a living sacrifice on the jade altar of the great god Mo. I, Wu Ling, priest on earth of the god Mo, shall myself make the sacrifice. Members of the Brotherhood, I have spoken. Take the pig from my presence and see that you keep him well. Let all prepare to leave at once. By night we shall be on our way to Kaitu."

So as Blake was dragged out of the apartment, Wu Ling and San disappeared behind the curtains at the upper end of the room, while the members of the Brotherhood stood with bowed heads in submission to the will of the Illustrious One.

When Tinker left Sexton Blake at the corner he strolled down to the docks to await the arrival of the two coastguards from Westward Ho! He had to put in nearly an hour before the motor-boat finally showed up, and when it had drawn in to the wharf Tinker hopped aboard.

From the two coastguards he got a detailed description of the two men who had come to Marsey Island and overpowered them.

From the description he had little difficulty in recognising Wu Ling and Baron Robert de Beauremon; and when the coastguards gave a detailed account of the great biplane by which they had come, Tinker's last doubt vanished.

It was not conclusive evidence, it is true; but in any prosecution which Blake might bring against them would be a very strong card indeed.

When he had got the coastguards to append their signatures to the report, he gave them a couple of sovereigns each, and saw them started back for Westward Ho! then he strolled back up to the town and made his way to the office of the chief of police. He found that gentleman had left for the day, and, finding his address, took a cab out to the house.

It was a fine old place, standing well in from the road, and surrounded by a high hedge, with a wide and airy entrance-hall, decorated with several large game heads. Into a small reception-room off this hall Tinker was shown, and a few minutes later the Chief of Police joined him.

In the first moment Tinker knew he could not have come to a better man. The chief—Featherstone by name—was a well set-up man, dressed in blue serge, which was set off by white spats. He was tanned to the colour of mahogany, and when at a later date Tinker discovered that he had been in India some years, reorganising the police methods there, he understood why the chief had the air he had.

He greeted Tinker warmly, sat down with smile of interest, when he discovered that he was Sexton Blake's assistant, and had come to see him on important business.

"Well, Master Tinker," he said, good-humouredly, "what can I do for you?"

"I hope a great deal, sir," replied Tinker. "I have come to see you

88

at the order of the guv'nor. He told me to give you all the details of the case, so with your permission, sir, I shall do so."

The chief drew out a cigar.

"Go ahead, my lad!" he said. "I shall be interested to hear what you have to say."

Forthwith Tinker began, and related all the details of the capture and release of the Munitions Minister. When he had finished that he went on to the escape of Wu Ling and Beauremon, and led up to the point where Sexton Blake had taken the daring course of going to the Chinese joint in order to try and get traces of Wu Ling.

"He wouldn't hear of any other course, sir," said the lad. "I tried to persuade him not to go, but he thought if he did not do so, but took ordinary police action instead, the Chinese might get wind of the fact. He wished to find out beyond all doubt if Prince Wu Ling were in Cardiff, or not. But he told me before he went to come and see you, sir, and to talk over with you what he wished done."

"And what is that Tinker?" asked the chief.

"It is this, sir. He wants you to get together some men, he said, either plain-clothes or special constables, and to hold them in readiness for action by midnight to-night. If he is not back at the Western Hotel by midnight, he wants you to raid this place to which he has gone, because he says only some serious complication will keep him later than that."

The Chief of Police smoked thoughtfully for a little, then he said:

"I shall certainly be very glad indeed to do anything I can, Tinker. I shall get together some men. Some of my special constables have been chafing for work lately, so I shall pick out a dozen from that force. I shall tell them to collect without badges or armlets at the Western Hotel at eleven o'clock, and we can wait there for Mr. Blake's return.

"If he hasn't come back by midnight you can lead us to the house and will raid it as he suggests. I have heard of Prince Wu Ling, and also Baron de Beauremon, but I did not dream for a moment that either of them might be in Cardiff. I shall be very pleased if we can rope them in.

"As far as this place you speak of is concerned, I know the house all right, and have had my eye on it for some time. But the occupants are most circumspect in their behaviour, and we have never before been able to get together sufficient evidence to raid it. To-night, with

Blake's lead, we have that opportunity, and you can count on us to do all that can be done. Is that satisfactory?"

"It is, sir," replied Tinker, rising. "I shall be at the Western Hotel at eleven to meet you; and at midnight, if the guv'nor hasn't returned, I can lead you straight to the house."

With that Tinker took his leave of the Chief of Police, and made his way back to the Western Hotel. He had done all he could now to guard against things going against Blake, and all he could do until the evening was to possess himself in patience.

Six o'clock drew round, and he went to his room to change into a dark suit. That done, he left the hotel and took a brisk walk. It was nearly eight o'clock when he got back to the hotel, but Blake had not returned, and Tinker cast himself down in the lounge with a heavy heart.

He felt moody and depressed, and seemed to feel a presentiment that things were not going well with Blake. Had it not been for Blake's express orders on the matter, Tinker would have been tempted to make the raid without delay. But orders were orders, and he would obey.

At half-past eight he went in to dinner, but could eat scarcely anything. A bite at this and peck at that, and he rose to seek the lounge again. There he kicked his heels until nine o'clock, and by that time was in a ferment of uneasiness.

As the minutes passed, without Blake putting in an appearance, his uneasiness deepened to a keen anxiety, and finally, unable to contain himself any longer, he got his cap and set off for a walk.

He walked and walked for the best part of half an hour, worrying over Blake and trying to make up his mind that he would be justified in disobeying orders this once.

But always, when he was tempted to do so, Blake's stern countenance rose before his vision, and he knew that he would not do so.

Finally, when night had fallen and the lights of the city were twinkling, he made his way along by the docks, where the bustle of day had given way to the damp mystery of night by the river front.

Unconsciously his footsteps led him to the wharf where he had met the motor-boat that day, and, by walking out to the end, he leaned against a mooring-post, very blue and very worried.

Sunk in reverie, he did not hear the almost noiseless swish, swish of something as it crept towards him out of the darkness, nor was he aware that ever since he had left the hotel the last time his every footstep had been dogged.

But the work of Wu Ling was thorough, and when he discovered that it was Blake, and none other, who had left the Western Hotel with a lad that day, he had lost no time in sending off the same Celestial who had brought the word to him in order to run Tinker to earth and kill him if a chance presented itself.

Foot by foot the creeping shadow drew nearer to the lad, the soft sound of the movements being lost in the guttural lapping of the black water against the wharf. Here and there were the lights of ships moored at the different docks, and in the channel beyond lay several steam craft, as though ready to leave at a moment's notice.

Tinker was idly watching a long, slim, rakish-looking craft which lay moored straight ahead of him when his uneasiness for Blake changed to a sharp feeling of premonition of danger to himself. Some instinct told him that in the darkness behind him a menace lurked, and with a slight shiver he straightened up, intending to return to the hotel.

Just as he did so, he gave a gasp as something came out of the darkness and hurled itself upon him. Tinker had just time to see that it was a Chinaman, with a bared knife in his hand, when they crashed together.

How he managed to elude the vicious thrust which was aimed at him Tinker never knew, but elude he did, and the next moment had sent his fist crashing into the face of the Celestial.

The other gave a grunt as the blow got home, but did not relax his grasp on the lad. On the contrary, he tightened it, and with a panther-like quickness wrapped one of his legs about one of Tinker's.

Tinker strove valiantly to break the hold, and to get his arms free for fist work, but the Celestial anticipated his every move, and held him like a vice while he worked the knife nearer and nearer to the lad's throat.

Some wayward gleam of light from over the water caught the bared steel and revealed the proximity of its menace to the lad.

With fascinated gaze, Tinker watched it come nearer and nearer, while he struggled wildly to get an arm free. He could feel rather than see the exulting gloat of the Celestial as the point of knife grew closer to its intended mark.

Then, just as the cold metal touched Tinker's flesh, he gave a frantic heave, and in the next moment both he and the Celestial went crashing over the edge of the wharf into the black water beneath.

In the fall their holds became broken, and when he came spluttering to the surface, Tinker's first act was to look round for the Chinaman. He saw him close at hand, and even as the lad turned to make for the wharf the other made for him.

Tinker saw that to attempt to climb up the wharf while the Celestial was so near meant certain death. On the spur of the moment, the only thing which presented itself to him was to swim out to the channel and, by outstroking the other, get sufficient lead to make a dash for safety. This plan he followed, and, turning on his side, struck out with a long side-crawl.

The Celestial was not to be thrown off so easily, however, for he made a sharp turn, and, sticking the knife between his teeth, set off after Tinker with a powerful overhand stroke which took him along at a rapid pace.

Tinker changed from his side-crawl to an Australian crawl, and struck out for all he was worth. Once he turned his head and looked.

He caught a glimpse of the Chinaman, with the knife between his teeth, coming hot after him. Then his plans merged into one idea—to find a landing-place as quickly as possible.

Then it was that he saw his present course would take him towards the long, rakish-looking craft at which he had been gazing from the wharf, and as he decided to make for her he began to shout for help.

For a hundred yards or so he kept the Celestial at about the same distance behind him, but then the lad's stroke grew a trifle slower, and from the sounds close in the rear he knew the other was gaining on him.

Again Tinker shouted for help, and this time he saw a white figure appear on the deck of the craft ahead. She was about fifty yards away from him now, and, giving another shout, Tinker put forth every ounce of strength.

The next moment he was almost blinded by a powerful white light which shone full into his face. The craft ahead had turned on her searchlight. It passed over Tinker a moment later, and rested on the Celestial, and there it remained.

So, in the golden path cast by the searchlight, the lad raced on, followed by the determined Chinaman, and just as he thought he must give up after all, a clear voice came from the ship saying:

"Keep it up! You will be all right!"

The following second he was conscious of a sharp crack overhead, and just as he went under, spluttering, a bullet tore through the air and struck the Chinaman full in the mouth, knocking the knife flying, and staining the water in front of him with deep crimson.

Tinker turned, and saw the Celestial throw up his hands and go under. Then he made another effort, and a moment later a rope struck him full in the face. He made a desperate grab at it, and, clinging on for dear life, was dragged through the water over the side of the ship and on to the deck.

To his utter amazement, a lovely face bent over his, and he was aware that Mademoiselle Yvonne was gazing into his eyes in stupefied amazement.

For the space of a minute or so, Tinker was in a fog of stupefaction. Five minutes ago he had been standing on the end of a Cardiff wharf, and had been attacked by a knife-thrusting Chink. Now his mind was telling him that he was lying on his back on the deck of a ship, with Mademoiselle Yvonne standing close to him.

It was unbelievable.

In an effort to come to a clear realisation of what it all meant, he moved his stiff limbs and got to his feet. Then he saw that the girl before him was no chimera of his imagination, but real flesh and blood.

Tinker passed a hand across his brow.

"I suppose it is you," he stammered inanely, "but I can scarcely believe it, Mademoiselle Yvonne."

Yvonne smiled.

"It is indeed I, Tinker," she replied. "But what on earth has happened to you? Why were you in the water at this hour of night, and why was that murderous Chinaman following you?"

At the mention of the hour and the reference to the Celestial everything swept back to Tinker's memory, and as he recognised the face of Hendricks, the mate of the Fleur-de-Lys, who approaching the spot where they stood, he laid a hand on Yvonne's arm.

"You must excuse my stupidity, mademoiselle," he said. "For a few moment I was a bit dazed. I swallowed some water, I guess. To find you here is a fortunate stroke. I am badly in need of someone with whom to talk over a serious matter."

"Is it about Mr. Blake?" asked Yvonne quickly.

Tinker nodded.

"Then you must get below and get into some dry things," went on Yvonne. "Hendricks, will you take him below and see that he is given some dry clothes? Then bring him to the saloon."

Hendricks came up now, and, after shaking hands with him, Tinker followed him along the deck and down a companionway to the officers' quarters. In the meantime, Yvonne went down the main companion to the saloon where Graves sat reading.

"What was it?" he asked, as Yvonne entered.

Yvonne lit a cigarette before replying. Then she said:

"It was Tinker."

For a moment Graves regarded her in amazement.

"You are joking!" he said finally.

Yvonne smiled.

"Am I?" she rejoined. "Wait and see!"

"But what is he doing here?" said Graves.

Yvonne shrugged, and shook her head.

"I don't know yet. It is something to do with Mr. Blake. He has gone to put on some dry garments, and will soon be here to tell us all about it. He was in the water, being chased by a Chinaman with a knife between his teeth. I do not know why. But let us wait until he comes."

Forthwith Yvonne strolled along to the small saloon piano, and, sitting down, ran her fingers lightly over the keys. She was still playing a soft reverie when Tinker came in, nor did she rise until she had finished it. Then, wheeling on the stool, she beckoned Tinker to come and sit near her.

The lad did so, and when he was ensconced in a low easy-chair, Yvonne said:

"Now, Tinker, tell us all about it!"

Tinker began, and related the germane points of the strange case which had brought him and Blake to Cardiff. But when he came to the part where Blake had decided to enter the Chinese joint and find out what he could, Yvonne tossed away the dainty Russian cigarette which she had been smoking, and leant forward tensely.

"Do you mean to say that, after what happened in the case of the Sacred Sphere, Mr. Blake went to this place disguised as a Celestial?" she asked quickly.

Tinker nodded.

"I tried all I could to prevent him," he replied, "but it was useless. You know what the guv'nor is when he has made up his mind to do a thing! One might as well try to move a brick wall with a feather! And it is now past ten o'clock. I have been worrying all the evening about him. I can't get the feeling out of my mind that something serious has happened to him. What do you think about it, mademoiselle? Do you think it would be safe to make the raid before midnight?"

Yvonne frowned thoughtfully.

"It would be the most sensible thing undoubtedly," she said at last. "But on the other hand, you have his clear command to make no move before midnight. Therefore I think the only thing to do is to wait until that hour. Don't you agree with me, uncle?"

Graves nodded his handsome head.

"From what I know of Blake, I should wait until the hour he himself named," he replied. "Undoubtedly it would be the most sensible thing to make the raid now. But still, orders are orders! and if an early raid happened to upset something he was just about to bring to a head, he would be greatly incensed."

Tinker nodded gloomily.

"I suppose that is what must be done," he said. "Any way, it is getting on for eleven now, and the police are to be at the hotel at eleven. At midnight sharp we will be able to make the raid."

"Will you excuse me for a few moments?" said Yvonne, rising suddenly.

Bowing to them, she slipped out of the saloon, and for a quarter of an hour or so Graves and Tinker talked indifferently. All the time the lad's thoughts were running on Blake, and the daring—ay, reckless—mission he had undertaken singlehanded, and he had no heart for anything else.

It was just five minutes to eleven, and he was about to ask to be set ashore when Yvonne re-entered the saloon. Both Graves and Tinker gazed at her in surprise. When Tinker had been dragged out of the water, and had looked up to see Yvonne bending over him, she had been clad in a soft, white evening-gown. Now that had been removed, and she wore a dark tweed costume, heavy boots, and a soft felt crush-hat.

She smiled as she saw their looks of surprise.

"Did you think you were going ashore alone, Tinker?" she asked gaily. "Come if you are ready. I am going with you, and the boat is waiting to take us."

Tinker jumped in.

"It is awfully good of you, mademoiselle," he said, "but really you mustn't think of coming with us to-night. It is no place for you."

Yvonne laughed softly, and for a moment her eyes grew tenderly reminiscent.

"Have you forgotten the past so soon, Tinker?" she asked. "Have I never been in difficult positions before?"

And Tinker, remembering the days when Yvonne's name had meant so much to a sensation-seeking Press, grinned, and said no more.

Graves rose and accompanied them as far as the deck where Hendricks and Captain Vaughan were waiting at the head of the ladder. At the foot of it a small boat rocked lightly on the black face of the water, and in it were four seamen ready to row them ashore.

Captain Vaughan greeted Tinker warmly, and, after a few words with his mistress, assisted Yvonne down the ladder. Tinker followed, and when they had taken their places in the boat the sailors pushed off.

It was only a few minutes before they pulled in at the foot of a flight of steps leading to the top of one of the wharves, and, helping Yvonne ashore, Tinker ran up the steps after her.

"You are not really intending to join in the raid, are you?" asked Tinker, as they walked up the wharf together.

Yvonne was non-committal.

"I shall hear what the chief of police says," she responded. "We shall have to hurry. It is past eleven now."

It was nearly twenty minutes past eleven when they finally walked into the lobby of the Western Hotel and approached the Chief of Police, whom Tinker saw sitting in a big easy-chair reading a newspaper. He jumped up as they approached and when Tinker had introduced him to Yvonne, said:

"I have heard nothing of Mr. Blake. Have you seen him?"

Tinker shook his head.

"No sir," he replied. "But, to be on the safe side, I shall just run up to our rooms, and see if he has come in."

He hurried away, and entered the lift. Yvonne sat down, and she and the Chief of Police talked until the lad returned. "He is not there,"

96

said Tinker, as he came up. "Nor has he been. If he had come in while I was out he would have left a note of some sort for me."

Yvonne turned to the chief.

"I suppose you will wait until midnight before making the raid?" she asked.

The chief nodded.

"I suppose so," he said; "but, to tell you the truth, mademoiselle, I do not like it at all. It strikes me that Mr. Blake has tackled a very risky business, and if it were any other man I should be tempted to go along at once."

"I think it is better to follow his instructions to the letter," remarked Yvonne. "At any rate, with your permission, Mr. Featherstone, I am going along with you."

"You!" ejaculated the chief, in astonishment. "Impossible, mademoiselle!"

Yvonne's white teeth came together as she set her chin determinedly.

"Nevertheless, I am going," she rejoined. "I have seen rougher places than this place will prove to be, and I know if Mr. Blake were here he would give his permission for me to go."

The chief raised his hands helplessly.

"If you insist, I suppose you must come," he responded. "Yet, mademoiselle, I can only think it is unwise. But it is twenty-five minutes to twelve. I think I shall gather my men together, and by then it will be time for us to go."

He excused himself then, and Tinker and Yvonne talked in low tones until he returned some ten minutes later. Then they rose and accompanied him out to the street where they saw four motor-cars drawn up at the kerb.

Even as they stood at the top of the steps the cars drew away one by one, and disappeared down the street.

The chief waved his hands towards them.

"There are twenty men altogether," he said, in explanation. "I chose them all from the special constabulary, and I think they are good men. I sent them on ahead, because we don't wish to arouse too much comment. Ah, here is my car now! Let us follow the others."

As a big touring car drove up to the kerb, they descended and climbed in. Then they started, and drove along the silent streets until they finally reached the Chinese district.

At the corner near the joint to which Blake had gone the car drew up, and, as they descended Yvonne and Tinker saw several men standing in the shadow a little farther up. The car in which they had come drove off, and they joined the waiting men in the shadow.

It was then the Chief of Police took charge of proceedings, and in the curt, business-like way in which he disposed of his force, it was plain to Yvonne and Tinker that he was an able tactician. Selecting his men four at a time, he spoke to them in low tones for a few minutes, instructing them what they had to do. Then, as one party disappeared up the street, he turned to the next.

Soon the whole force of twenty men had faded into the shadows, and, pulling out his watch, the chief held it so Tinker and Yvonne could see it.

"It lacks only one minute off midnight," he said. "Come, let us walk up the street! It will be just midnight by the time we reach the rendezvous, and then we shall make the raid. It is hopeless for any of the inmates to try to escape, for my men have the whole place completely surrounded. As they dash out we shall rake them in. But I do wish, mademoiselle, that you would stand in a place of safety."

Yvonne laughed softly, and, thrusting her hand beneath her jacket, drew out a small, wicked-looking automatic.

"I can protect myself." she replied. "I wouldn't miss this for worlds, and, besides, Mr. Blake is my friend, and I fear he must be in danger."

Nor did she add that within her was a keen sense of anticipation of excitement which had swept over her the first moment she had set eyes on Tinker, which could not be assuaged until with her own eyes she had seen that Sexton Blake was safe.

For Yvonne was Yvonne, and in yielding her girlish heart to the masterful personality of Blake, had brought that into her life which would never go out of it while she lived and breathed.

He it had been who had loomed up before her in the past like some rock of refuge—like a beacon of hope. Time and again when, during the progress of her vengeance against the eight men who had swindled her mother and herself in Australia, Blake had crossed her path, she had fought out her fight, the while she stared up into the darkness at night trying to put from her mind, and to hurl from the pinnacle which he held in her heart, the man of strength, and yet of unyielding hardness.

Hope had blazed brightly at times, and, lying wide-eyed in her dainty white bed, while the Fleur-de-Lys tossed gently on the ocean swell, or dipped her nose into the caressing waves of the South Pacific, but always the reaction had come.

Then, as Blake had given all but the one thing she desired—his love—she had withdrawn into herself, and, in her girlish pride, has assumed towards him a coldness which her throbbing heart denied vehemently.

And Blake! Even Blake, wrapped up though he might be in his profession, had not failed to realise what had happened. With the sweet radiation of her love he had stood cold and unresponsive; and yet, when it had been withdrawn and locked up within Yvonne's breast, he, man-like, had missed something, and had felt a tugging at his heart-strings which he did not—could not understand.

Something was missing—something which unconsciously he had found very sweet. There were occasions, too, when a very fiend incarnate was roused up in Blake.

In all his life he had never experienced such a feeling of blind rage as sometimes seized him of late. And, strange to say, this feeling came over him only when Yvonne's smiles and Yvonne's sweetness were given to another.

Tinker, shrewdly observant, watched these new moods of his master's and kept his peace; but, young though he was, he read the mystery, and could feel with the master he loved so in the stern fight he was having. It was the age-old struggle between the profession which is all in all to a man and first insidious coming of the tender influence of a good woman.

And Blake, clever though he might be at probing the mysteries of others, and putting his fingers on the weak spot in the armour of the criminal, was strangely obtuse when it came to analysing his own feelings. Something was upon him which he did not understand. It remained to be seen if realisation would come to him. If it did, no man could foresee the result.

So it was with all this memory of the past in her mind, and the present fear in her heart for the man she loved, that Yvonne slipped forward through the shadows towards that dark house of eternal night and mystery. Foot by foot the trio crept forward until they were within a few feet of the door. Then the Chief of Police paused, and, raising a whistle to his lips, blew a triple signal.

Instantly men seemed to swarm from every direction, and, as the cordon drew in the chief made for the door, followed by Tinker and Yvonne. The Chief turned the handle, but, as he expected, the door refused to yield; then, raising his hand, he knocked loudly.

Again and again he knocked, but no reply came. The house was in darkness from top to bottom, even the saloon on the corner being closed and shuttered. The whole atmosphere of the place was brooding and menacing, and, when in response to his summons the chief received only silence, he called two of his men.

Then, standing back, they rushed the door, and burst it in with a crashing and splintering of wood. Into the dark hall the party rushed, lighting the way with electric pocket-torches. Through the hall and into room after room they went, searching here and there for any signs of the occupants of the house, but on all sides there met them only a weird, uncanny emptiness.

At last Tinker and Yvonne, who were together, came to the opium-room, where only that day the besotted figures of the drug fiends had tossed in delirium, but now the mattresses contained not a single human form; the attendant was not to be seen, and only the stale odour of the drug hung all over.

The Chief of Police joined them.

"I have called in all my men," he said curtly, "there doesn't seem to be a soul about the place. They must have received warning of the raid, and made good their escape."

And, though they literally tore the place to pieces, they could find not one skulking Celestial in all that rabbit-warren.

Beaten and disheartened they returned to the opium-room. To say that Tinker was worried was to put it mildly. Blake had come to that place during that afternoon, when, as the lad knew, it was full of habitues. Now, after only a few hours, they found it empty and deserted.

What did it all mean? What could it all mean? There was something very sinister in that desolation about them.

Where was Blake? He had told the lad that if he had not returned to the Western Hotel by midnight a raid should be made, and his absence would mean something had gone wrong. But never such a situation as this had Tinker contemplated.

That Blake was going into the jaws of the Yellow Tiger was certain—that those same jaws might close upon him had been anticipated by both, but that there should be nothing visible by which to follow the fate of his master—there the lad was at a loss.

The Chief of Police was equally at a loss. He stood within the opium-room his keen eyes searching out every hole and corner of the place, the while his men ransacked the house from top to bottom.

Soon they began coming in with their reports. One man had penetrated the upper part, and there had come upon room after room empty of human beings, but littered with all the curious paraphernalia of the place. Others returned from like excursions to the bar, and the rooms off it. But as far as Sexton Blake was concerned they could see not a single thing to offer any suggestion as to what might have become of him. He had apparently vanished into thin air, and each one of those who stood there knew what fate he had gone to.

It was when the last of his men had returned to report that there was no-one about the place, that the Chief of Police turned to Tinker and said:

"Well, my lad, I fancy Mr. Blake has miscalculated this time. We followed his instructions to the letter, and came at the time he said. You have seen what we found. Unless you have some suggestion to offer I am afraid there is nothing to do but to draw off my men. I have had my eye on these people for a long time, as I told you, but they are slick, as they have proved. If I can get my hands on them I shall rope them in quickly enough, but they apparently have some very complete system of underground information, for it is beyond all doubt that they received warning of an intended raid."

Tinker nodded moodily.

"I can think of nothing else just now," he said slowly. "I am much obliged to you for what you have done, sir. But the fact remains that the guv'nor is in their hands, and he must be found. I know Prince Wu Ling, and I know how he hates the guv'nor. If he is in the hands of the Chinks they will kill him as certain as the sun will rise to-morrow. And they will see that he suffers torture before he dies. Wu Ling has had his game queered too often in the past to be lenient. Nor would the guv'nor buy his freedom at any price Wu Ling would ask. No sir, I shall have to think of something to-night."

With that they turned towards the door with the intention of making their way back to the street. It was not until then that Tinker and the Chief of Police noticed that Yvonne was no longer there.

They turned in some surprise as they noticed her absence, and

Tinker, raising his voice, called:

"Mademoiselle! Mademoiselle!"

There was no answer, so, with a word to the chief, Tinker turned back towards the opium-room to seek her.

Just as he did so there was a distant call, and the lad recognised Yvonne's voice. It was full of urgency, and as he dashed back through the opium-room the chief followed him.

Pausing half-way down the room Tinker called:

"Where are you?"

"Here!" came the distant reply. "Follow the opium-room door to the door at the end, and open that. Then come along the passage."

They ran to the door, and, jerking it open, dashed through into a corridor. Along this they sped until suddenly they came to a door of an open room. Inside was Yvonne, and as they appeared she beckoned to them.

"Come at once!" she said. "I have made an important discovery!"

They entered the room, and, standing just within the door, gazed at their surroundings. Lit up by pocket-torches the room looked small and dingy enough, and in no wall was there a window. It was simply a large box, and from the fact that it contained scarcely any furniture they guessed rightly that it might have been used as a room of detention for any fractious habitues of the opium-room. A table, a chair, a rough pallet on the floor, a small mirror, and the most primitive sort of washing utensils comprised the furniture of the room, and as they gazed upon it both the Chief and Tinker wondered what important discovery Yvonne could have come upon in such a place.

A moment later, as they went forward to where she stood by the table, they found out, for she lifted the mirror from the hook on which it had been hanging and held it out to them.

"Read what is written on it," she said, in a low tone.

Tinker took it and held it so they could see the surface plainly. At first they saw only a very dirty surface covered with the dust of months, perhaps years, but as the light of the electric-torch picked out the lines on the surface, they suddenly became aware that in that dust there was a message scratched.

Eagerly they bent to read it, and as they took in its import grew very grave. This is what they read:

"I must have been followed here. Have been discovered and overpowered. Am prisoner in this room. Have been up before B. of Y.

B. (which Tinker immediately knew mean the Brotherhood of the Yellow Beetle), and death sentence passed. Will not be killed here. Am being taken to Kaitu as sacrifice. Follow.—B."

Slowly they made their way from the room and walked back to the street. There the Chief of Police told off three men to remain on guard at the joint, and, sending for his car, drove Tinker and Yvonne back to the Western Hotel. As he said good-night to them he laid a hand on Tinker's shoulder.

"Rest assured, my lad, I shall do all in my power to get track of these people, but for the present I see little that can be done beyond watching and waiting."

Tinker said nothing, but, when the Chief had driven off, turned to Yvonne.

"I will not rest in such a state of uncertainty!" he cried. "Something surely can be done—something must be done to find the guv'nor."

Yvonne laid both hands on his shoulders.

"Something will be done," she answered softly. "Come! Let us go to the Fleur-de-Lys and make our plans."

So together those two, who loved Sexton Blake, hurried towards the wharves to form a scheme for his rescue—if they were not already too late.

CHAPTER 7   The Voyage to Kaitu

In order to get a true perspective of the predicament in which Sexton Blake found himself it is necessary to make some attempt to realise the true calibre of Prince Wu Ling. Wu Ling, a man of the East, and one whose whole life had been dedicated to a single great purpose, could in no way be termed an ordinary criminal, if indeed the name criminal might be applied to him at all.

True, in the furthering of his aims, he did not hesitate to apply every known form of pressure, but what he did was at no time done with the spirit of criminality born of a desire for material gain. Of money, of power, of adulation he had more than falls to the share of ordinary man.

Nothing which criminality could yield could swell one iota those material advantages which were his.

The star to which he had hitched the waggon of his ambition was the one which would drag along through its course the great yellow race until it was high over all the races of men, and until the white races, which Wu Ling looked upon as interlopers and arrogant pretenders, were driven into the abyss of annihilation.

Therefore, when he be regarded from this perspective, it can be seen that his hatred of Sexton Blake was not the hatred of the criminal for the enemy of crime, but the hatred of the fanatic for the one man who, more than any other, had continually risen up to stand in the way of the successful prosecution of the plans of the Brotherhood of the Yellow Beetle.

That being so, Wu Ling could conceive of no more fitting fate for Blake than he should go to form a living sacrifice to the golden god Mo, the patron of the Brotherhood of the Yellow Beetle, and the god to whom, more than any other, Wu Ling paid his worship.

Sexton Blake it had been who, in the days when Prince Wu Ling first appeared in Europe to propagate the ideal for which he stood, had always risen to confound the Oriental in his doings. Not only in Europe, but in the whole of the world—ay, even in China itself had Blake come to grips with the yellow man, and on nearly every occasion had his wits proved more inventive than those of the Easterner.

Then had come that awful meeting in the island of Kaitu, when he and Wu Ling had rolled on the sand locked in a deadly embrace,

104

each fighting to encompass the death of the other. It was a fight never to be forgotten by either. When after an eternity of straining Blake had got his fingers on the throat of the yellow man and had exerted all the strength at his command, Wu Ling, too, had got home, and there they lay, each praying that his own power of resistance might last the longer.

Blake's last recollection had been the sinking of his senses into a great gulf of blackness, and as he had passed into oblivion it had been with the thought that Wu Ling had conquered. But he had come out of that eternity of night to find Tinker bending over him and to be told that he had killed Wu Ling. Yet that he had not killed this man Blake was to find out some time after, and the discovery was to be but the prelude to a renewal of the old struggle.

Now, through all the criss-cross paths of the past, he had fallen into the hands of the enemy and from that grip he had little chance of escaping.

After Blake had been before the Council of Brotherhood in the den in Cardiff, he had been thrown into the small room, where some hours later Yvonne was to find the message, which, in his utter desperation, Blake had scrawled upon the dustladen mirror.

After that two Celestials had come in to him, and before he could prevent them, had shot the point of a hypodermic-syringe into his arm. With the plunger pressed home, Blake knew that nothing he could do would off-set the action of the insidious drug which was in the needle.

Though his natural power of resistance caused him to fight hard, he gradually sank under the influence of the drug until be became comatose.

His next cognisance of life was when he awoke in a dark and stinking hole, to find his legs and face in the runway of scores of rats, and to one of the bites of the filthy rodents was his waking due. Rats—the pests of man, bred in filth and carriers of the worst diseases, dirty and squealing cowards when well fed, vicious and deadly when hungry.

To Blake, coming slowly to his senses, it seemed that there must be millions of the rodents making a rendezvous of his body. Body after body flashed over him, giving off that filthy rodent odour as it passed, and, even in his semi-conscious condition, nauseating him at the thought of the vileness they breathed.

But where was he?

Bit by bit his wits collected and massed into their place, until, with a strong effort of will power, he sat up and stared into the stygian darkness which surrounded him, trying to piece together the broken fabric of memory.

Slowly it came upon him that there was a vile odour which was quite distinct from that of the rodents, which, with his coming to himself, had fled shrieking, to stand off at a safe distance and regard him. Not that he could see them, but he could feel them, which was a thousand times worse.

How long a time had passed since he had been drugged in the room at the Cardiff den he could form no conjecture. It might have been a day or week—he could not guess.

As his thinking machinery began to work more smoothly, he gradually became aware that the strong odour which he had noticed was familiar, and then suddenly if flashed upon him what it was. It was the smell of rotten bilge-water, which meant that he was aboard ship. But where—and bound for what port?

With that came the memory of his sentence at the hands of the Brotherhood and the ruling of Wu Ling that he should be taken to Kaitu as sacrifice to the golden god Mo. Then Wu Ling had had his will, and he was at sea bound for the East, where his fate would be slow, but none the less sure.

There, in the blackness of the hole, Blake thought of Tinker and his last words to the lad before he went into the jaws of the tiger. He had been most emphatic in his instructions, and if the lad had followed his orders, which he knew would be the case, then at midnight of the day when he had gone into the joint, there must have been a police raid.

If that were so, why had he not been found? Had he been spirited away from the place before the raid or had the police come, and had they perhaps passed within a few feet of him? He could not tell.

Next he began to puzzle over the weak spot in his plans which had led to his discovery. That it was nothing to do with his disguise he was certain. It was too perfect for that.

How had it come about? He could not even make a guess, for he did not know of the sleek Celestial who had seen him leave the Western Hotel in the company of Tinker.

Nor was that all which gradually formed in film of fancy as he sat chafing his sore joints and gazing into the darkness. He had a vague recollection of the face and voice of Beauremon—Beauremon, whom he thought had dropped out of the game after the affair of Marsey Island.

Somewhere during the blank of the immediate past Beauremon must have been in evidence before the fog of oblivion seized him, for Blake was certain his memory was not playing him tricks. But where or how he could not place.

As a matter of fact, he was right, for in the small room at the Cardiff joint where he had received his quietus, Beauremon had come in just as Blake was growing unconscious.

What Blake did not know was that there was discord in the camp between Beauremon and Wu Ling—discord, the cause of which was Blake himself. Beauremon had joined with the prince in the kidnapping affair, and when that had failed, had, in accordance with his agreement, stuck to the game.

He had not been present when sentence had been passed on Blake, but when invited by Wu Ling to go with him to the East, and there join in the prosecution of further plans of the prince's, he had consented. Only then did he discover the fate intended for Blake; and whatever his faults, Baron Robert de Beauremon proved for once in his life that he still had some trace of decency left.

Wu Ling had told him coldly and unemotionally that Blake was a prisoner and was bound to the East with them to form a living sacrifice to the golden god Mo. Beauremon had protested vehemently, but what could he do?

There he was alone on a ship, which, while it was disguised as an ordinary tramp, was really the private yacht of Wu Ling, and which was manned by men every one of whom was pledged to the service of the prince.

For once in his life Beauremon was absolutely helpless to do anything, and, realising how dangerous his own position might become did he rouse Wu Ling's antagonism, he said nothing more. Yet he did not forget that he was a white man—one of the inevitable breed.

Even as Blake lay crouched and sore in the hold of that ship were Wu Ling and Beauremon talking in the saloon above, and the result of their conversation was an order from Wu Ling to bring the prisoner on deck.

To Blake a faint square of light showed overhead as the hatch was removed, but he did not shift his position until he saw two dim figures approaching. To save being kicked to his feet he struggled up, and swaying heavily, allowed himself to be dragged along to the ladder.

There he summoned up all his will power for the ascent, and, clutching the iron rungs of the ladder, began to climb. What a ghastly torture that ascent was! It was no easy feat for a cool-headed, sober man to climb one of those narrow ladders, with a ship swinging and plunging to the dip of a heavy sea, but with a brain reeling to the sheer edge of unconsciousness, with the arteries throbbing with a fierce overcharge of blood, and with every bone and joint aching painfully, such a journey was the quintessence of exquisite torture.

But Blake made it, despite the handicap under which he was struggling, made it because he would undergo anything rather than suffer the indignity of being assisted up by either of the coolies who had been sent down for him.

Once on deck he reeled against the side and almost collapsed. The fresh breeze which was cutting across the port quarter refreshed him like a draught of sparkling wine, and from his brain the fog slowly cleared.

He was not given long, for was not the Illustrious One waiting for him? The two coolies caught him by the arms, and, dragging him along the waist of the deck, hoisted him up the after-companion and along to the companion-way which led down to the main saloon.

There, sitting at the large table which ran almost the full length of the saloon, he saw Wu Ling with Beauremon beside him.

As the hold of his two conductors relaxed, Blake drew himself up and stared coldly at Wu Ling. For a long minute the two stared back at each other, then Blake shifted his gaze to Beauremon.

To the latter he spoke sneeringly. "So you have turned renegade, have you, Beauremon?" he said, "one would have thought you might have done a little better than that."

Beauremon, who was smoking a cigarette and trying to look nonchalant, could not help a flush of anger or shame. He withdrew his cigarette as though to speak, but Wu Ling forestalled him.

"You will reserve your remarks for me," he said curtly. "Baron de Beauremon has nothing to do with you. He is my ally at present, and had I given him his way, you would not be bound for the island of

Kaitu. He has the heart of a chicken."

Blake flashed a quick look at Beauremon and saw the latter give an almost imperceptible nod. In a moment it was all clear to Blake. He could reconstruct in imagination the argument Wu Ling and Beauremon must have had regarding him, and if what Wu Ling said was true, then he could only think that Beauremon had put in a plea for leniency.

Undoubtedly the baron had no qualms about Blake being killed, but that he had not consented to the British gentleman being offered up as living sacrifice, caused a glow of respect for Beauremon to rise up in Blake.

He turned back to Wu Ling.

"Well," he said coolly, "why have you sent for me? Have you decided to give me more decent quarters?"

Wu Ling shrugged.

"What matters it where you rest?" he said. "You will soon be beyond caring about such things."

"I have not yet been placed on the altar," replied Blake, "and until then I am very particular about such things. After I have gone as a sacrifice to this god Mo of yours will be time enough for you to talk of other things, and then I shall not be interested. In the meantime I should like some clean linen, a decent bunk, and some food."

Wu Ling made a gesture.

"Silence!" he ordered. "I did not have you brought here to discuss such things. I brought you here because Baron de Beauremon has put forth a suggestion, and which, if you fall in with it, will entitle you to meet death in a different way, and not go as a sacrifice to the blessed god Mo."

"So Beauremon has been bargaining for me as much as he can," thought Blake. "Rather decent of him, at any rate." Aloud he said: "Well, what is your proposition, Wu Ling?"

The prince leaned forward a trifle.

"I have this to offer you, Sexton Blake. Reflect well before you answer. Nor think that anything can save you. That you shall die I am determined, but if you do as I wish, I am willing to concede to you the choice of death you are to meet.

"It was you who ruined my plans regarding the Munitions Minister. It is you who can do something towards retrieving that position. I want from you a letter written and signed by you asking the

Munitions Minister to meet you at a place where I shall name.

"It will be necessary for that meeting to take place at sea, and an urgent letter from you will cause the Munitions Minister to come. If you agree to that I will return to British waters, and when the Munitions Minister has come will let you choose your form of death. Or, if you are then prepared to swear that never again will you oppose me, no matter what behest you may receive, I may—I say I may consider your release unharmed. What is your reply?"

Blake stared at Wu Ling for a moment, then suddenly he burst into laughter.

"And think you I would listen to any such proposal as this?" he asked.

"You have much to learn, Wu Ling. You will get no letter from me to the Munitions Minister, beyond one telling him where you are and asking him to send a gunboat to blow you out of the water. That is my answer to your proposal, and it is final."

Wu Ling for once showed a gleam of anger in his eyes, but he made no reply to Blake. Instead, he beckoned to the two Celestials who stood by the door waiting.

"Take this man and bind him well," he said curtly. "Throw him back into the place from which you brought him. Leave bread and water there and see that it is given to him once a day. It will be sufficient to keep him alive until we reach Kaitu, and then we shall go to the god Mo as I ordered. You see, Baron de Beauremon, what profit we have found in your proposal."

Beauremon said nothing, but flashed a look of sympathy at Blake, who smiled back, and then, as the two Celestials approached, turned to meet them.

He held up his hands as though in readiness for his bonds, but as they reached out for his wrists, Blake suddenly withdrew them, and, doubling up his fists, struck twice in rapid succession.

Down they went one after the other, and then, before Wu Ling could rise or call out, Blake was upon him.

Like a tiger he leapt across the table, crashing full upon Wu Ling, and they went down together.

Blake realised that he had little time to spare. In a few moments the whole ship's crew would be upon him, and he could not count on Beauremon as an ally. The baron might try to get Wu Ling to be more lenient in his intentions regarding Blake, but he would scarcely take the part of Blake against the man with whom he had thrown in his lot for a consideration.

It was Beauremon's boast that when the Council of Eleven took up a matter they stayed by it until it was finished. Therefore, Blake knew he must play a lone hand.

As he and Wu Ling went down, the prince tried hard to reach something which was beneath his tunic. Blake seeing, or rather feeling, the motion, rolled quickly over, and then shot his own hand beneath the loose jacket of the Celestial.

Almost at once his fingers touched the butt of a heavy automatic, and with a sharp pull he had it out. Without the slightest hesitation he clubbed it and brought it down with all his force full on Wu Ling's head.

No cranium ever owned by man could have withstood the force of that blow. Wu Ling gave a grunt and lay still, and Blake leaped to his feet just as Beauremon jumped for him.

Again raising the automatic, Blake struck hard, catching the baron square in the centre of the forehead. A ridiculous look of surprise appeared for a moment in the Baron's eyes, then his legs collapsed and he dropped to the floor, to lie in a heap across Wu Ling.

Blake now made for the door and raced up the companion-way. Once on deck he stood for a moment to get his bearings. Over on the port side was a boat, and towards this he sprang. That something was amiss was now evident to the crew, for several of them appeared in the waist and started towards the poop.

Blake disregarded them for the time being, and devoted all his energies to the purpose in hand. Reaching the boat he unfastened the falls, and, straining hard, pushed it out. Then he let it go, and it ran down from the davits with a rush.

At the same time one of the Celestials whom he had knocked down in the saloon, rushed up on deck screaming something in Chinese. Whatever it was, it electrified the crew, for as one man they rushed towards Blake, drawing their knives as they came.

Blake turned to meet them, and, levelling the automatic, pulled the trigger time after time.

Man after man went down, but the others kept on, and Blake, who had no extra clip of cartridges for the pistol, saw that he must retreat.

Firing a last shot at the leader, and sending that Celestial to the deck, he sprang for the side, and catching hold of the ropes, slid down to the boat.

Bending, he released both the falls, and, as the boat became free, it dropped swiftly astern.

As the ship passed him, Blake looked up, and saw several of the crew gathered at the side ready to hurl their knives at him.

A moment later the hail of steel started. Blake dodged and ducked. Then the bulging stern of the tramp swept by, and he dropped out of range of the knives. But he knew this respite would not be for long. As soon as Wu Ling recovered, he would issue orders for the chase, and in a little open boat, on a sea of which he knew not even the name, what chance had Blake?

Slender though the chance was, Blake determined to make full use of it. Dropping to a seat, he picked up the oars, and began to pull with all his might. He cared not which way he went or how. His sole idea was to put as much space between himself and the tramp as possible.

Even as he settled down to hard work, he saw her swing round, and Wu Ling standing at the side.

Still he rowed and rowed as he had never rowed before, and he covered the best part of a mile before the tramp came round close enough for him to see what was afoot. Then it was that he saw half a dozen Celestials standing at the side, with rifles trained on him.

"Never mind!" he muttered, as he continued to strain at the oars. "Better to die this way than the way Wu Ling intends, and I swear they will not take me alive! They will have to shoot me full of lead first!"

The next moment the bullets began to fall about him. At first they went beyond him or to one side, falling into the water with sinister little plunks, but when the marksmen had the range, they began to hit the boat.

One struck the bottom in the bow, and as it tore through the wood Blake saw the water spurt in through the hole made. A second struck the starboard oar, and, ricochetting from it, plunged through the bottom. Another hole, through which the water began to bubble, had been made.

Then a perfect hail of lead struck the boat, falling all about him, splintering the sides and the oars, but so far miraculously missing him.

Still Blake pulled at the oars in a race which, if it lasted much longer under those conditions, could only end one way. But the ingrained grit of the white man kept him at it. Then he saw that he must block up the holes some way, or the boat would sink under him.

Drawing in the oars, Blake searched about in the bottom of the boat for something which would serve his purpose, but could find nothing. In desperation he tore the shirt from his body, and, ripping it into strips, rolled them up to form plugs for the holes.

While the bullets still fell about him, he worked strenuously, stuffing the material into first one hole, then the other. It was a poor makeshift at best, but it all was all he could do.

From under the stern sheets he took a battered tin can which he found there, and began to bale furiously, there was still a good deal of water slopping about in the boat when he desisted, but he saw if the plugs held as they were he could keep ahead of the incoming water.

Taking up the oars once more, he started to pull again; but, as he leant back, he suddenly paused and gazed at a great black pillar which was apparently joining sea and sky in the east.

From the appearance of the water and the feel of the air, Blake had formed a shrewd opinion that he was very far indeed from England. He knew that he had probably been kept drugged for days in the hold, and perhaps for weeks, but not until he saw that black pillar before him did the truth flash upon him.

Then he knew that while he lay unconscious in the hold of the tramp it had come many, many leagues. And in truth it had, for they had rounded the Cape days ago, and at the moment when Blake had been dragged to the saloon they were ploughing through the Indian Ocean towards Java and the passage into the China Sea.

The black pillar was the forerunner of a cyclone.

As he realised the full portent of what it meant, Blake drew in the oars again, and bent over the stuffing he had placed in the holes.

He knew, if he were caught by the force of the hurricane, that his little boat would be tossed about like an eggshell, yet he would do what he could.

At the same time, he saw that the tramp had also seen the oncoming menace, for she had sheered off suddenly, and was steaming at full-speed towards the north-east.

It was hard to choose between being in the open sea in a leaking boat while a hurricane approached and on board the tramp in the clutches of Wu Ling, but as Blake saw her drawing farther and farther away, he knew that at least one enemy was out of the way for the present.

How he worked in those next minutes! Frantically he pulled out the stuffing and screwed up the material into balls as tightly as he could make them. Then he pressed them back into the holes, and when he had filled the last, set to work again to bale.

Blacker and blacker grew the pillar in the east. Then came a first ominous puff of wind. It was followed by another, and then there arose a low, booming sound, the meaning of which Blake knew only too well.

Almost before he could catch hold of the seat and cling on for dear life, the hurricane swept upon him, and as the little boat was tossed skywards in a boiling cauldron of foam the fleeing tramp became blotted out from his view.

Of what followed during the next few hours, Blake to this day has only a vague idea. It seemed to him that there was an eternity of tossing and pitching, with a devil's wind catching him by the throat and threatening each moment to crush him to death beneath its weight.

He had a hazy recollection of baling mechanically with one hand while he clung on wildly with the other, of pitching and tossing yellow waves which curled upwards, huge as houses, and came crashing downwards, threatening to swamp the boat each moment, of wild roarings and boomings as the hurricane tore its way across the ocean, and of sheets of rain which came down in pelting, driving, cutting lines.

He was alone, it seemed, of all humanity in a tossing sea of yellow terror. And yet he knew that he must have caught only the tail-end of the hurricane.

How long this went on, he did not know. He only knew that he baled incessantly, and that it seemed that he had been condemned to bale yellow water for eternity.

Then the hurricane subsided and the rain passed, to leave him tossing about helplessly on the sweep of the battered ocean.

Gathering his wits together, Blake stopped baling, and took stock of his condition and that of the boat. The oars had gone in the first wild swoop of the hurricane. One of the seats was smashed, and the stuffing had come out of several of the holes.

Now the water was literally pouring into the boat, and as he again took up the bailing, Blake knew that it was a losing fight. Still he persisted, and as night came down, it found him still at it.

The last thing he did before darkness caught him was to gaze about the horizon. No sign of the tramp nor of any other ship did he see. Then he returned to his bailing.

What a ghastly, fever-haunted night it was! The strain through which he had been had left him constitutionally weakened, and nourishing food had not passed his lips for days.

A man cannot exist on bread and water and stand up under a situation such as Blake was in. It takes solid food basis to stand being pitchforked into such a place, and solid food Blake had not had.

Fever got him about midnight. Delirium followed, and while he baled he sang—sang the wildest, craziest songs which ever came out of forecastle.

Hour after hour he baled and sang, shrieking forth the pirate songs of old to a black and lowering sky.

Morning found him still at it, burning with fever and squatting up to his waist in water. How the boat ever kept afloat was a mystery. She was nearly full of water now, but through the fever of his delirium there came to Blake the idea that he was beating the creeping water. It lent him fresh energy—the energy of delirium, for which his system would pay dearly.

The grey clouds gave way, and the sun came out. Still the crazed man in the boat kept up his exertions, but by noon his fever-stricken brain snapped, the outraged body went with it, and Blake—a shrieking maniac—collapsed into the water which almost filled the boat.

Slowly but surely it crept up and up and up, until it had him by the throat; then the yellow water swept completely over the gunwale, and the man was carried out of the sinking boat into the grip of the waves.

Some instinct impelled the whirling brain to telegraph an imperative message to the limbs of the man. His arms and legs moved, and mechanically he began to swim.

Up to the crest of a roller he went, then down into its lap, tossing aimlessly and without cognisance, but still keeping afloat.

And with the embrace of the water came a change in his condition. The voice broke out once more, cracked and hoarse, but still expressing the madness of the brain. No song went croaking across the waves this time, but the delirious mutterings of the helpless maniac.

Of Tinker he mumbled and gurgled—of Tinker and the case they were on. Somehow his brain conceived the idea that Tinker was lying on the altar to be offered as a sacrifice to the golden god Mo, and that he was bound and helpless to release the lad.

How he cursed and raved as he, in fancy, watched Wu Ling, in the yellow robes of a priest of Mo, approach and lift the gleaming knife which would give the lad's blood to the god.

Then it seemed as if Tinker suddenly changed to Yvonne. It was she who lay on the altar, victim to the god.

As Blake, in fancy, saw her helpless beneath the squatting god, his frenzy redoubled, and, raising his arms, he thrashed the water madly, calling down upon Wu Ling curses which would have frozen the blood of a sea pirate.

In his frenzy he seemed to succeed in breaking his bonds and tearing them from him, rushed for the altar. Wu Ling, with upraised knife, reached for the white pillar which was Yvonne's throat, and, turning to Blake, smiled.

Blake hurled himself forward, and seized upon the bare blade of the knife. Then his tortured brain collapsed entirely, and, with Yvonne's appealing eyes upon him, he dropped into a pit of darkness.

Then the mocking waves seized upon him and bore him onwards—ever onwards!

CHAPTER 8   Yvonne's Rescue

Never had the Fleur-de-Lys had a harder chase than the one she undertook when Yvonne and Tinker boarded her at Cardiff, and set off down the Bristol Channel after the ship which they knew must be somewhere not very far ahead of them. Nor was there any need of a spur to cause everyone on board to do his utmost. Yvonne, to whom, each member of the crew rendered the most implicit obedience—an obedience born of love for the "little missie"—wished it, therefore, it would be done.

From Captain Vaughan, on the bridge, to sour old MacTavish in the engine-room, each man put forth his best, and the high-powered engines of the Fleur-de-Lys pounded mightily as she tore down the Channel, and headed for the Atlantic.

Until the yacht had dropped into Cardiff for supplies she had been doing special work for the Admiralty; but Yvonne arranged a release from these duties, and now the yacht was free to go wherever her mistress willed.

Across the Bay of Biscay they raced, ever on the watch for a tramp steamer, for in Cardiff Mr. Featherstone had discovered that only one ship had cleared for China within the time that Wu Ling must have gone, and that ship was the tramp steamer, Boca Tigris.

Off Finisterre, a British T.B.D. hailed them and released them, but before they tore on again they were in possession of the information that the Boca Tigris was ahead of them.

Not until they were off Gib, did they discover that no ship by that name had attempted to pass through the Straits, which meant that she had gone on past the Canaries, and intended reaching the Indian Ocean by way of the Cape.

Once more the course was changed, and south they raced as fast as the Fleur-de-Lys could take them.

They stopped at Las Palmas long enough to take in coal and fresh provisions then on again, past the Cape Verde Islands, which rise, barren and forbidding, off Cape Verde, and so into warm current which falls down the West Coast of Africa.

No stop was made from Las Palmas till they reached Cape Town, but there they still had no word of the other ship. Yet they knew she had not gone through the Mediterranean, and, since she had been ahead of them as far as the Straits, she must have gone by the Cape.

Even Wu Ling would not take the time necessary to cross the Atlantic and round Magellan, while it was unlikely they had tried the Panama Canal. Therefore, Captain Vaughan reasoned that she had kept well out from the regular track of ships, and for that reason they had not had word of her.

At Durban his reasoning proved correct, for there they passed the word with a small whaling steamer, which worked out from the Durban whaling-station, and she reported that she had signalled a tramp named the Boca Tigris only the day before, and that the tramp was heading under full steam towards the north-east.

That was enough for those on the Fleur-de-Lys. Up the Indian Ocean they raced on the new scent, so to speak, with Tinker, Yvonne, and the crew of the Fleur-de-Lys keeping a sharp look-out.

Nearly four weeks of steady steaming they had done, and still no sign of the quarry. From the grey waters of the north had they come, passing down through the blue of the Tropics round the Cape, and up into the warmth of the Indian Ocean. All zones had they been in, and yet that elusive tramp kept just ahead of them.

Then one evening they held a Council of War, and it was decided to continue on to Java, and to stop at Batavia in order to try and get some further news of the tramp, which they knew must be bearing Sexton Blake to his doom.

The very next day came a terrific hurricane, which threatened to annihilate them, and for ever prevent them from reaching the object of their journey. It was the same storm which swept down upon the tramp and upon Sexton Blake, who was even then tossing about in the small boat which he had taken from the Boca Tigris.

For several hours the barometer had been falling steadily, until Captain Vaughan ascended the bridge wearing a very worried look. He knew the Indian Ocean well, and he knew of old those sudden storms which gather somewhere off Ceylon, and sweep across the ocean to beat themselves out against the shores of far Africa, or, in some instances, at the head of the Persian Gulf. He knew also the absolute necessity of running for it, and abandoning the chase if he would save his ship.

With the coming of the menacing, black cloud in the east, he had not hesitated. The Fleur-de-Lys had been made ready, as far as possible, to meet the shock, and when it came she was sent dashing into the very teeth of it.

118

Hour after hour the hurricane raged, tossing them this way and that like a cork upon the breast of a giant cauldron, and hour after hour did the staunch little yacht wallow her way through the awful seas.

Then the storm passed on its way west, and, with the lessening of the awful strain to the yacht, those on board began to take stock of their condition. All that evening, and all night they ploughed their way onward towards Java, and at midday the following day took an observation. They found that the storm had blown them nearly a hundred miles out of their track, and that they were well east of the narrow entrance to the Java Sea.

Up on the Bridge another Council of War was held in the afternoon. While Captain Vaughan stood by the man at the wheel, Yvonne and Tinker joined him and together they discussed what should be done. Captain Vaughan and Graves, who had also come up, were for returning to England, and in his argument the captain used some convincing words.

"It is this way missie," he said. "The tramp was ahead of us when the hurricane struck. It is just possible that she made the Java Sea before the storm rose. In that case she would have escaped it entirely. If so, she is well on her way up the China Sea by now, and will reach Kaitu before we can get into the China Sea. In that case, we will be too late—well, to put it bluntly, to save Mr. Blake. It is not easy to give up after such a long chase—but what else is there to do?"

"The captain speaks sense," said Graves. "We will never be able to reach Kaitu in time. Wu Ling's tramp had more speed than we reckoned on. They will make Kaitu to-day or to-morrow at the latest, if they missed the storm."

Yvonne held up an imperative hand.

"Wait!" she commanded. "I have no doubt that you, uncle, and you, Captain Vaughan, are speaking with reason, but, at the same time, there are other things to be considered. We must know that Mr. Blake was taken away on the tramp, and that he is to be offered at Kaitu as a sacrifice to the idol Wu Ling worships. Do you think, even if we are late, that I will go back to England, and permit that to be carried out without a fight? If you do you are sadly lacking in proper knowledge of me. We are his only hope. Shall we desert him? Did he ever desert me or you when we depended on him? Did he return to London and say it was useless, when I myself was in the hands of Wu

Ling? It is only a short time since you, uncle, appealed to him for his aid when I went down to Kilchester Towers. Did he refuse you? No! He came down himself to Kilchester Towers, and remained there until he had cleared up matters. And will I desert him now? Is that what Yvonne would do? If it were, then I should never again hold up my head.

"Whoever wishes to leave the yacht may do so at Batavia. I have doubt that they can easily get passage back to England from there. But as for me and the Fleur-de-Lys, it continues on to Kaitu, and, if anything has happened to Sexton Blake, then may heaven help Wu Ling and his gang, for I swear I will harry him off the seas and off the earth, if it is the last thing I do! That is my word, and that is what shall be done!"

The two men who were the recipients of Yvonne's anger, stood aghast at her outbreak. She looked very regal and very beautiful in her rage, and Tinker, who had listened eagerly to her words, gave a soft "Bravo!" as she finished.

Graves and Captain Vaughan started to speak in reply, but, with a gesture, Yvonne silenced them, and then suddenly her blue eyes filled with tears. She turned away hastily, and started to descend from the bridge, but Captain Vaughan caught her by the hand.

"That's all right, missie," he said soothingly. "I didn't know you felt that way about it. There ain't no one on this yacht that will go ashore at Batavia, but every hand goes on to Kaitu; and if you want to blow the place out of the water, it shall be done. I know—" But just then the captain was interrupted by a voice forward.

"Something on the port bow, sir," came the cry.

With the instinct of the seaman, Captain Vaughan turned at once, and, snatching up a pair of glasses, raised them to his eyes.

Yvonne had turned back at the cry, and waited beside him.

"I can't make out what it is," said the captain, lowering the glasses. "If it didn't seem impossible, I would say it was the body of a man or an animal."

Quickly Yvonne took the glasses, and trained them on the object which was being tossed up and down by the waves.

For a long minute she looked, then, lowering the glasses, she said:

"Get out a boat at once! It is a man!"

Laying down the glasses, she climbed on to the rail. Captain

Vaughan leapt forward to stop her, but he was too late, and a second later Yvonne, placing her hands over her head, had cut the air like an arrow, taking the water cleanly.

They saw her come to the surface, saw her arms rise and fall in a strong overhand stroke, then saw her draw nearer and nearer to the floating object beyond.

Tinker, who had heard her cry, hurried away to have a boat lowered, and as it took the water he was first in it. Half a dozen men tumbled in after, and away they went at top speed towards the swimming girl.

She reached the object on the waves before they reached her, and, as they came up, they saw her arms cradling the thing which Captain Vaughan had said looked like a man or an animal.

Into the boat they dragged first the body of the man whom Yvonne held, and then Yvonne herself, and, as he bent over the wet, sodden, and unconscious man who lay at his feet, Tinker uttered a sharp exclamation.

Unless he had gone stark, staring mad there before him was, or rather was what he had once been, Sexton Blake.

The next moment there was a little gulping sob, as Yvonne, the tears streaming from her eyes, collapsed in a heap, her arms outspread over the body of Blake.

CHAPTER 9   The German Submarine

Sexton Blake was not dead, though he had gone perilously near the valley from which there is no return. Once back on board the Fleur-de-Lys he was put into a steaming bath, then wrapped in warm blankets and put to bed.

Nor would Yvonne hear of even Tinker nursing him. It was she who sat beside him hour after hour—it was she who held his hands while he tossed and raved in a mad delirium—it was she who heard from those loosed lips the full story of his suffering as he raved wildly—it was she who thrilled at the mention of her own name and locked within her breast the secret maunderings of a tortured mind.

And it was Yvonne whose lips shamelessly and softly pressed his and soothed him to rest. To her had come the urgent need to do for Blake.

How her heart, which for months had carried its own sweet secret, thrust aside the bars of restraint and burst forth in a paean of happiness, only she herself knew.

But those long hours which she spent beside that fever-stricken man would remain with her all her life as a bright dazzling stretch of achievement.

It was the need to serve which a woman feels for the man she loved. And Yvonne loved Blake.

Hour after hour she nursed him, watching incessantly while the fever ran its course, and eagerly awaiting the hour when sanity should return. It did return, thanks to Blake's iron constitution, and when, weak and exhausted, he opened his eyes to meet hers, he could only stare feebly at the wonder of it all.

He had gone into darkness while being tossed about by the waves—he had awakened to sanity and warmth to find Yvonne bending over him. And then, with happiness singing in her heart, Yvonne went out and called Tinker.

It is no part of this story to pry into that meeting between Blake and the lad. Sufficient is it to say that when Tinker emerged his eyes were wet, and he sought a quiet corner of the deck, there to give thanks for the great gift which had been theirs.

But hard on Blake's recovery things began to happen which needed the wits of everyone on board to cope with. It had been tentatively decided to change the course of the Fleur-de-Lys, and after

122

putting in at Colombo to make for England. But Fate was determined that they should not do so.

She still had things in store for them which would need all their nerve and courage to handle, and it was perhaps as well that they did not know all that was to happen during the next few hours.

The first intimation that anything was wrong came from the man on look-out, was sighted a steamer on the starboard bow. She was ploughing along at a good speed, and the way she was running would bring her close to them. Then Captain Vaughan, who was on the bridge, made out her name, and with that the excitement arose on deck.

It was the Boca Tigris. That she had seen the Fleur-de-Lys was evident, for she came straight towards them, and after a hurried consultation they decided, in view of Blake's condition to make a run for it.

Captain Vaughan signalled the engine-room for full speed, and while the smoke belched forth from the yacht's funnels he changed her course.

Away they went racing west with the tramp after them, but they soon saw that they were to have no easy escape.

It was then that Wu Ling proved the tramp to be far different from what she seemed. Their first intimation of this was when a dull boom broke out behind them, and a shell whistled overhead, to fall in the water close to them.

To reply was useless. The Fleur-de-Lys, while armed, had no heavy guns, the largest being a Maxim, and what could a Maxim do against a gun which could throw a shell two miles? So they continued to run for it, while the Boca Tigris ploughed along after them, firing from time to time.

It was half an hour before the first hit was registered, and then the funnel of the yacht was struck fair and square. It split asunder with the force of the explosion, tearing loose as it went, and creating havoc on deck.

Another shell struck forward and burst just in front of the forecastle. Three men were struck by the flying bits of shell, and while Tinker went down to keep Blake from worrying, Yvonne went to look after the wounded men.

Captain Vaughan had now adopted a zig-zag course in order to spoil the aim of the gunner on the other ship, but a shell which struck the side of the bridge as it passed showed how well the enemy had the range.

It was a losing race and all hands began to realise it. Then, even as the Fleur-de-Lys shivered beneath the shock of another shell, did a long, slim, grey shape appear on the surface of the water and cut across towards them.

The firing from the Boca Tigris stopped at the same instant, and like those on the yacht, all hands looked to make out the nationality of the submarine which had appeared so suddenly.

From the bridge Yvonne gazed at it through the glasses.

After a few moment she spoke.

"It is German I am certain," she said. "Ah! Someone is coming through the opening in the conning-tower. It is—I am certain it is German. Hendricks! Get out the British flag and break it out at once."

Yvonne now turned the glasses in the direction of the Boca Tigris and saw that the tramp had come up rapidly, and that already the Yellow Dragon of China was flying from her stern.

The submarine had apparently disregarded the tramp, and was drawing in closer and closer to the yacht. Then the British flag fluttered bravely and defiantly from the stern.

Hard on that the man who had come through the top of the conning-tower on the submarine reached down, and taking a megaphone from someone below, raised it to his lips.

"Ahoy! Fleur-de-Lys!" he shouted, in strongly-accented English. "You are British?"

Captain Vaughan looked at Yvonne, and when she nodded he picked up the yacht megaphone.

"We are British!" he called back. "Who are you, and by what right do you hold us up?"

"We are German," came back the reply. "We give you ten minutes to get out your boats. At the end of ten minutes we blow you out of the water."

To run for it was out of the question. To fight was equally useless. There lay the submarine close to them, and each one on the yacht knew that a torpedo was in her tube ready to be discharged. They could only submit, much as it hurt.

Turning to Captain Vaughan, Yvonne gave the word, and a moment later the old seaman, angry at being humiliated, called out to the crew to lower the boats.

While Hendricks the mate went down to the engine-room, Yvonne hastened to tell Blake, and Tinker superintended the lowering of the boats. Captain Vaughan was busy getting together the papers of the yacht.

At the head of the companion-way Yvonne came upon Blake leaning weakly against the handrail regarding the submarine.

"I heard everything," he said, as she came towards him. "There is nothing else to do. It is too bad. I am ready."

"You shouldn't have come up alone," Yvonne admonished him, her eyes filling as she saw his weakness. "Come! Let me help you."

Taking his arms, she assisted him to the side, and there Blake descended into one of the waiting boats. The rest of the yacht's company soon came over the side, filling the other two boats, and when all were in them they pulled away from the side.

Lying off a short distance they lay on the oars waiting to see the last of the Fleur-de-Lys. But for some reason the torpedo did not come, and gazing at the submarine they saw that she was signalling to the tramp.

A moment later a boat put off from the tramp and made for the submarine, and as it danced over the waters the explanation came to Blake. Yvonne was in one boat while Tinker was in the other, and Blake and Hendricks in the third. Blake bent over to Hendricks and said in a low tone:

"While they are busy watching that boat approach the submarine, tell your men to row round to the other side of the yacht. I want to go aboard."

Hendricks stared at him for a moment and looked as if he would speak, but something in Blake's manner decided him to do as he was requested. He gave the order to his men, and unobserved by the others they pulled round the stern of the yacht.

When the boat had been brought in close to the side Blake got up, and gathering all his strength made his way to the deck of the yacht.

There he paused and leaned over.

"Have them pull back, Hendricks," he said. "We don't want to arouse suspicion. I will manage to reach you somehow."

Hendricks, who was trained to obey, gave the order, and as the boat pulled away again Blake made his way along the deck.

He staggered more than once as he went, for he was still very weak, but sheer will-power held him up and he kept on. At the foot of the companion, leading to the bridge, he paused to gather his strength together again, then on up to the bridge deck.

There he turned, and making his way along to the wireless room, kicked open the door.

It was only a forlorn hope on which he was bound, but he was determined to try it, and if he went to the bottom with the yacht while doing what he could to save the others, he would not mind.

Seating himself at the instrument he tuned up, then placing the receivers to his ears started to send the S.O.S.

Time after time he tapped it out, waiting at intervals for a call, and hoping against hope that it would come before the enemy discovered what he was about.

Even while the hope flared strongly in him he heard the tramp of feet along the deck, and a few moments later he saw half a dozen vicious-looking Chinese rush for the wireless-room.

Dropping his left hand to his pocket, Blake jerked out his automatic and levelled it. A bullet came crashing towards him and struck the table close to him.

He pulled the trigger of the automatic. It barked out again and again, and two of the Celestials went down.

Then, holding the rest at bay with the weapon, he began again to send. From somewhere across the water came the reply, and Blake discovered to his joy that he was being answered by a British ship of war.

He sent out an urgent message for help; then, just as he had almost completed it, a bullet struck the key of the instrument and put it out of action.

Staggering to his feet Blake kicked the door to and locked it, then crouched beneath the window to wait for the next rush. And while he crouched there he wondered what had happened since he had come aboard.

Much indeed had taken place, and had he but dreamed what it was he would have thrown open the door and risked death.

The boat which had gone from the tramp to the submarine had borne Wu Ling and Beauremon, and there they had convinced the German commander of the submarine that they were indeed working hand in glove with the Germans.

When Wu Ling showed papers which proved the truth of his statement and requested that certain of the yacht's company be handed over to him, the German commander was only too pleased to do so.

So it was that the boats from the yacht had been surrounded, and with the deck gun of the submarine pointing at them, Yvonne and Tinker had been forced to climb over the gunwale into the boat from the tramp.

A search of all three boats failed to reveal Blake. No one had seen him go aboard the yacht except those in Hendrick's boat, and not twenty submarines would make them tell.

Wu Ling, shrewd as always, speedily guessed the truth, and rushing his two prisoners aboard the tramp, sent his men back to drag Blake off the yacht.

But Blake's message had gone and not even Wu Ling guessed that the answer had come from a blunt-nosed British T.B.D., whose smoke was at that very moment rimming the horizon.

She was coming up hand over hand, and while Blake held the wireless room against the attacking Celestials, succour was nearer than he thought.

He emptied his pistol once, hurriedly thrust in a fresh clip and emptied it again, just as the enemy made a fierce rush.

Though Blake got several of them, they succeeded in reaching the door of the wireless room, and it strained inwards as their weight was thrown against it. Then across the water there came the low wail of a siren—once, twice, thrice.

Almost immediately Blake heard the rush of feet as the attacking party raced down the deck. At first he thought it was only a ruse, but as no further attack came, he risked a peep out, and saw that the deck was clear.

Opening the door, he stepped out on to the deck, and, going to the side, was just in time to see the German submarine sink below the surface.

Turning, he gazed in amazement at the tramp. She was already under way, heading north as fast as she could go, and then, looking south, Blake saw the reason.

Scarcely a mile away was the British T.B.D., coming on the scene as quickly as her powerful engines could drive her. Tossing about on the waves were the three boats from the yacht, and as he saw them Blake essayed a feeble cheer.

Little did he dream that Yvonne and Tinker were not in them, but instead were prisoners on the tramp which was racing north at top speed.

As he appeared at the side, Hendricks gave an order to his men, and they pulled in close to the yacht.

Blake swarmed down to the small boat and tumbled in. Then, while they pulled towards the other boats, Hendricks told him what had happened.

Blake's eyes grew sombre as he listened, and his hands clenched fiercely.

"If I had only dreamed it!" he muttered, when the mate had finished. "Wu Ling has played a winning card, and Heaven only knows what fiendish fate he will think out for them! Nor will it be any the less because he has lost me. But the T.B.D. will be able to overtake them, and then—wait until I get my hands on Wu Ling!"

By this time the T.B.D. had come close, and the boats pulled in to them. In a few words, Captain Vaughan recounted what had occurred, and then he and Blake were invited to come aboard.

There Blake related the whole story, even from the time the Munitions Minister was kidnapped, and as he listened the young commander of the T.B.D. set his jaw grimly.

"So that is the game—is it?" he said, when Blake had finished. "Well, I'll tell you what I will do, Mr. Blake. I will go after that tramp, and if she refuses to heave to, I will let her have a shot or two. Do you care to come with me?"

"I should be very glad indeed to do so," replied Blake. "The Fleur-de-Lys could follow as quickly as possible."

So it was arranged, and soon the crew of the yacht were back on board, with MacTavish and the stokers in the engine-room, getting ready to give the Fleur-de-Lys all she would take.

Captain Vaughan was on the bridge, and as the T.B.D. raced away north after the tramp, Blake waved his hand to the gallant old seaman.

An hour passed—two hours—and they began to gain perceptibly on the tramp. Then Fate gave them another blow, for, as the afternoon waned and the commander of the T.B.D. expressed his hope of overtaking the other ship before night fell, a thick bank of cloud came down from the Java Sea and swallowed all the visible world within its damp maw.

CHAPTER 10   Rogues Fall Out

It was a hot night on the Island of Kaitu, as steaming day, with the jungle sweating hard, and not a breath of wind in from the sea, had presaged the night which had come. For once the night breeze had not come down from the hinterland, and over the lagoon and village which lay close to it the heat pall of the day still clung.

On the narrow, fringing coral reef beyond the lagoon, the surf rolled in lazily, murmuring incessantly, and rousing thoughts of cool depths. In the lagoon itself, the water lay still and limpid, its glassy surface broken only by the glow of phosphorescence as a school of fish struck the medusa and spread it apart.

Through the paw-paw trees and cocoanut palms, which lined the edge of the lagoon, lay the village, and from it came a low constant hum as of many voices. Now and then the wail of the temple bell broke out, calling through the night to those who would hear. Then its jangle would die away and silence reign once more.

In the lagoon lay a single ship—a small tramp steamer—and on her stern was painted the name Boca Tigris. For the Boca Tigris had made Kaitu safely, and on this night—the same night of the day which had seen her arrival—there was much to be done. The Illustrious One had come back to his own, which was a great event in itself, but rumour had it that he had brought two prisoners.

It was said by some of the priests that the blessed god Mo would receive a human sacrifice before the night was over, that the sacrifice would be a white man, and that the Illustrious One himself would perform the sacrificial rites. Hence the constant murmur of voices which came through the trees.

From the jungle near the edge of the lagoon appeared a man. He stood for some time gazing out at the tramp which rode at anchor in the best holding ground of the lagoon. Then he turned and made for the trees.

As a slanting beam of moonlight struck his face, it might have been seen that he was no Celestial, but a white man, and some would have recognised him as Baron Robert de Beauremon, of Paris and New York and London. But what a different Beauremon from the usual suave and nonchalant man who was well-known at the International Club of London!

On this occasion his eyes were filled with trouble; his usually

129

immaculate dress was all awry; his hands twitched nervously as he swung them at his side.

He looked as if he had gazed into the mirror of his own soul, and had not liked what he saw there.

For be it known Beauremon and Wu Ling had arrived that day in Kaitu by the Boca Tigris, bringing with them the prisoners which by the grace of the commander of the German submarine they had been permitted to take—Mademoiselle Yvonne and Tinker.

With Blake lying in the hold of the tramp, Beauremon had made a protest; with Tinker in the grip of the Yellow Tiger, he would have been content with a similar objection. But from the moment he had laid eyes on Mademoiselle Yvonne, things had assumed a far different perspective.

Not that the Baron Robert de Beauremon was any sentimentalist. Far from it! He was the head of the Council of Eleven, which organisation had carried out many daring and conscienceless affairs since its inception. He was not so much immoral as simply unmoral. He didn't know what morals were.

When he had formed the Council of Eleven, he had been world-weary. He had tasted of the sweets and bitters of life, and found them not satisfying. In the Council of Eleven, he found the constant excitement which his blase nature craved. Nor had he flinched from any deed in the carrying out of his purpose.

That type of nature, combined with the wealth which was his, had made him all the more dangerous. But never before had he been up against exactly this type of proposition.

He had joined in with Wu Ling in the Island of Marsey, off Pembrokeshire, for a certain consideration. He had done his part in bringing things to a successful issue.

When Sexton Blake had outwitted them, he had still stuck to Wu Ling. He had sailed with him for the East, and, to do him credit, had objected strenuously to the offering of Sexton Blake as a sacrifice to the god Mo. But, as is already known, he had been ruled down, and for the time being had submitted.

But when Yvonne had been brought aboard the tramp, Beauremon had looked once into her eyes, and his fate was sealed. It had come home to him exactly what he was doing, and with that realisation had come the decision to have an understanding with Wu Ling.

When they had gone ashore in Kaitu, he had sought the prince in his quarters behind the temple, and there had stated his case.

"It is no good, Wu Ling!" he had said bluntly. "I will not stand for this sort of game! I am pretty bad, I know, but I cannot bring myself to lending a hand to any such thing as you contemplate. With all due respect to you and your Royal blood, you are yellow and your prisoners are white. Therefore I wish to know your exact intentions regarding them."

Wu Ling shrugged and said:

"I saw you when you looked at the white girl this morning, baron. I have been expecting some such objection on your part. It is strange that you should have these scruples after seeing the girl. But you will be unwise to attempt to baulk me in my plans. I gave you an opportunity of leaving me before we sailed from Cardiff. You elected to remain."

"That was because I felt I had not fulfilled my contract with you," broke in Beauremon.

"That is neither here nor there," resumed Wu Ling. "I tell you now that I will brook no interference from you. As to what my intentions are, I will tell you. To-night, at the moment when the moon has reached its zenith, the boy shall go to the altar in sacrifice for the golden moon god Mo. The girl—the girl, baron, goes to my harem."

"And I say these things shall not be done!" burst out the baron.

"So?" had replied Wu Ling softly. "And who, pray, will prevent me?"

"I will!" the baron had replied, and therein he had made a great mistake.

Wu Ling had shrugged, and, with a wave of the hand, had dismissed him, and Beauremon, wishing to think, had gone out from the temple to plan against the prince.

But Wu Ling was not the man to have an avowed enemy loose on the sacred island of Kaitu, and when Beauremon had gone forth from his presence, two Celestials had slipped along after him.

Into the jungle had the baron gone, carrying with him the memory of the two eyes of morning blue into which he had gazed, and after him had gone two yellow executioners.

A hundred yards from the temple they came upon him and attacked him. Beauremon had been taken by surprise, and had he attempted to fight would have been cut to pieces in a few seconds.

The orders of the assassins had been to see that he did not return. But Beauremon, knowing something of Wu Ling and his methods, had taken to his heels, and had dashed on blindly through the jungle, with the two Celestials after him.

Without any sense of direction had Beauremon run, and it was probably this which saved him, for at the end of half an hour, when he had staggered out on to the edge of a high bluff overlooking the sea, he had shaken off his pursuers.

All that afternoon he had lain there, gazing out to sea, and trying to think of some way by which he could save the girl who was in the grip of Wu Ling.

With the coming of evening he had ventured to leave his retreat and make his way down to the edge of the lagoon, and so it was that, while Kaitu panted and gasped beneath the lingering heat of the day. Beauremon ventured forth from the concealment of the trees.

It would be some time before the moon reached its zenith. As yet it had only come up above the gaunt peak which rose in the centre of the island, striking the water of the lagoon slantingly, and causing a path of gold which stretched clear out to the narrow entrance, which lay between dank bunches of stinking mangroves.

Though he had thought and thought for hours, Beauremon had been able to hit on no plan whereby he, single-handed, might overcome the forces against him. Yet was he determined to release Yvonne, and if possible Tinker, before Wu Ling should have had his will with them.

So much to his credit.

It was with this aim in view that he started for the village, where he knew must by now be gathered every inhabitant of the island, to witness the sacred ceremony which preceded the offering of human sacrifice to the god Mo.

At the very edge of the paw-paw trees, he paused and gazed out across the lagoon at something which was stealing in through the mangrove-lined passage.

For a few moments he stood there thus, scarcely daring to believe what his eyes told him he saw; then, turning, he stole back down the beach to the very edge of the water.

Again he paused, watching the grey shape which had come through the passage resolve itself into the blunt lines of a ship of war. And then, as she dropped across the path cast by the moonlight,

Beauremon saw that she was the same T.B.D. which had put the tramp and the submarine to flight the day before.

What did it mean? Before he had time to answer his own question, his attention was attracted by a noise in the direction of the tramp. He, himself, knew that only one man had been left aboard on watch, and now as he saw a boat being lowered he knew that one man had also seen the sinister, grey shape steal into the lagoon, and was off to warn Wu Ling.

Beauremon screwed up his eyes, and watched the progress of the small boat as it came shorewards; then, when it was still halfway between the tramp and silvery beach of the lagoon, he stepped into the water and plunged, cutting the surface with scarcely a sound.

Swimming easily, he headed for the small boat, and, as he drew nearer, saw the Chinese watchman, who had been left aboard the tramp, rowing with short, powerful strokes.

It was evident that a severe panic had seized upon him. Yet he could have no suspicion of Beauremon, for he knew nothing of the split between the baron and Wu Ling. Nor did he have any suspicion for when Beauremon drew near the Celestial eased up, and in Chinese said:

"There is danger, Excellency. The Illustrious One must know."

Beauremon laid a hand on the gunwale of the boat, and drew himself over the side.

"The Illustrious One will know," he said shortly. "I myself will tell him."

While he was speaking, he was drawing nearer and nearer to the unsuspecting Celestial, who was still resting on the oars.

Then suddenly Beauremon sprang on him, and the startled Chink went down with his mouth open ready to yell.

But the baron jammed his clenched fist into the aperture, and the cry died off with a choking gurgle. Beauremon followed up the jab with whole weight of his body, and, getting one knee in the pit of the Celestial's stomach, he began to exert a gruelling pressure.

The Chink gasped and wriggled and fought like a tiger; but Beauremon was out for quick work, and, using his left, sent in blow after blow to the other's face.

There could be only one result—there was only one result. Under the hail of blows the Chink doubled up and collapsed, and Beauremon, jamming him into the stern of the boat where he could watch him, sat down and took to the oars. Then, turning the boat, he sent her skimming across the lagoon towards the grey shape of the T.B.D.

As he drew near he saw several forms at the side, and, pausing in his rowing, he called softly:

"Are you there, Sexton Blake?"

Immediately came the reply:

"Yes. Who is it?"

"Beauremon," replied the baron. "Throw over a ladder. I want to come aboard."

Instantly a ladder was thrown over the side, and, pulling in the oars, Beauremon clutched it, running up easily.

Once on deck he saw by the light of the moon that four men had gathered at the top to receive him, and that foremost among them was Sexton Blake. Yet there was something concerted in the way that quartette of hard-bitten men stood which made Beauremon smile.

It was evident that they were taking no chances of treachery. And when Blake spoke, it was plain that he was decidedly suspicious of the baron's coming.

"Why have you come here?" asked Blake curtly.

The baron leaned against the side.

"I suppose on the face of it my visit must look decidedly suspicious," he replied coolly. "But I shall be as brief as possible in my explanation. To jump all that happened in England, let me begin at the point where you were sent for by Wu Ling on board the Boca Tigris. Wu Ling himself told you, I think, that I had interceded for you, Blake?"

Blake nodded.

"That is true," he said coolly. "Proceed, please."

"Then your attack on Wu Ling came, and you almost brained him. If you will remember, I did not lift a hand to help him, though you next attacked me, and nearly finished me. Is that true?"

"Is it true," said Blake.

"You succeeded in getting away," went on Beauremon. "You know what happened after that. I have spoken of the other things in order that you may try to appreciate the position I was in. I was trying to keep my contract with Wu Ling, and yet I would not consent to some of the programme he had outlined. The appearance of the German submarine was a great surprise to me as to you. I knew nothing of its coming—neither did Wu Ling. Then, while Wu Ling went across to the submarine to explain matters, you managed to get aboard the yacht, and send a wireless message for aid. The crew of the tramp, which had been sent to recapture you, were held off by you at the point of the revolver, and the appearance of this T.B.D. on the scene forced Wu Ling to recall them before they had effected your capture.

"But he managed to get possession of Tinker and Mademoiselle Yvonne, and managed also to drive through the Sunda Straits into the Java Sea, and on up the China Sea to Kaitu without being overtaken. Nor does he dream yet that you are here. There are great doings in Kaitu to-night, and it is for that reason you see me here an apparent traitor to Wu Ling. Today I thrashed out matters with him. I would not consent to the programme he had outlined, particularly regarding Mademoiselle Yvonne."

"And what is that programme?" asked Blake tensely.

"It is that Tinker shall go to the altar as a sacrifice to the god Mo, and that mademoiselle shall go to join Wu Ling's harem. That is what brings me here. I informed Wu Ling that it must not be. He insisted on it, and I left his presence. But I did not go alone. Two of his henchmen followed me, and tried to knife me in the bush. I escaped from them, and made my way through the jungle. I lay hidden all day, and this evening I ventured down to the beach in order to devise some plan for rescuing the two prisoners. It was then I saw your boat steal into the lagoon, and that I realised that you had come in the nick of time. While I stood there I saw the watchman put off from the tramp to warn Wu Ling. I swam out to meet him. He did not suspect me, and I overpowered him. He lies below in the boat at this moment. That is my story, and that is why I am here. After all, I am a white man, and I cannot bring myself to countenance what Wu Ling intends this night. You can believe me or not."

Blake stepped forward, and, bending his head, gazed deeply into Beauremon's eyes.

"If I thought you were laying some trap for us, I would kill you where you stand!" he said tensely. "But if you are telling the truth, then, Beauremon, you are more of a man than I thought you were. Look me in the eyes and answer me!"

The baron lifted his head, and gave back look for look.

"I swear by the eyes of Mademoiselle Yvonne that I speak the truth!" he said, in a low tone.

Blake's hand shot out, and they gripped.

"I believe you," he said. "If you could take that oath and perjure yourself, you would be a skunk!" Then Blake stepped back. "Gentlemen," he said, turning to the three officers who had stood close by, "now that I am satisfied as to the intentions of our friend here, let me present him to you. Baron Robert de Beauremon—Commander Porter—Lieutenant Trepwitt, and Midshipman Fortescue."

When the three had shaken hands with Beauremon, Blake turned back to the baron.

"You said, baron, that there were great doings afoot in Kaitu to-night. Do you know at what hour Wu Ling has planned them?"

Beauremon looked across the limpid waters of the lagoon, which was being stirred ever so gently by the first caress of the coming night breeze, then his gaze travelled upwards to where the great stars rode supremely beautiful.

Raising his hand, he pointed towards the moon.

"They take place when the moon reaches zenith," he said, in a low tone.

Immediately all eyes were riveted on the great disc which hung like a glorious golden globe over the jagged summit of Hani-Ku, the towering peak which rose from the centre of Kaitu.

"When the moon reaches the zenith," they murmured, one by one, "and that will be inside an hour."

CHAPTER 11   The Last of the Temple

Beauremon had made no mistake when he said that there were great doings afoot on Kaitu that night. Up in the temple the priests had been busy all day, feeding the flames of the fire which burned at the foot of the great statue of the god Mo, and preparing the ceremony which would take place that evening.

In the room at the rear of the temple Wu Ling had spent the entire afternoon in prayer and meditation. Outside, the people of the village moved about restlessly, waiting for the word to come forth that the Illustrious One was ready.

What a barbaric scene it was. The temple—a miniature of the great one in Peking—standing with its front to the east, facing the eternal coming of Morn. Within the huge statue of the Buddha, which rose at the rear, its outlines silhouetted against a tracery of palm-branches which could be seen through a large semi-circular opening which looked to the west.

All round the temple the beautifully carved scenes of the life of Confucius and the Buddha stood out clear and distinct, even in the mellowed light of the temple.

The floor was antique mosaic of the finest, and the panels of the walls themselves were covered entirely by goldleaf.

To one side was the alcove where stood the altar to the god Mo. It was a richly-decorated place, covered with mosaic and goldleaf, and lit up ruddily by the light of the censers, which burned night and day.

On a jade base sat the god, a huge figure of pure gold, whose eyes were blazing emeralds. At the foot of the figure was the great block of porphyry hewn, and polished by hand, on which the sacrifices were made.

Usually these sacrifices composed the bodies of white kids—young goats—specially bred for the purpose, and once a month when special invocations were made to the god was a white bullock slain. Be it noted that always the sacrifice was white.

Those who have read the classics of the ancients, those who have enjoyed the beautiful poetry of Homer in the "Iliad" and the "Odyssey," or followed the adventurous voyage of Aeneas, when after the fall of ancient Troy he took his father Anchises and his little son Ascanius to seek a new home for the remnants of the Trojan race, will recall the consistency with which the ancients made sacrifices to their gods. Then the gods were Jupiter—Juno, Neptune, Venus, Mercury, and Minerva, and a host of others.

They will recall, too, when Aeneas, after passing through many stirring adventures, after leaving the shores of Ilium, and passing the Cyclades as well as the terrible Harpies, to be finally shipwrecked on the shores of Africa, made his prayer to the gods, and later on, when, after his sad dallying in the new city of Carthage, he finally reached Italy, he made sacrifice of white bullocks.

In some way the sacrifice of white animals to the god Mo must have descended from those ancient times, or in the past have been contemporaneous with them. Perhaps the idea travelled from China to ancient Troy. Who knows?

At any rate, it still persisted in the worship of the god Mo, but with the difference that on occasion a human sacrifice—if white—was also demanded by the ritual. Therefore, it will be understood how great was the excitement on Kaitu, when it became known that a living sacrifice would be made to the god.

At the very moment when the moon rose over the jagged edge of Hani-Ku, Wu Ling emerged from the room of meditation at the rear of the Buddha.

After making a short prayer there, he rose and passed on to the alcove where squatted the god Mo. Once more he prostrated himself, and for a long half-hour remained motionless, while six priests of the order, in robes of yellow and white, knelt behind the altar awaiting the pleasure of the great high priest.

Finally, Wu Ling rose, and, approaching the sacrificial altar, gazed upon the fire which burned there. Then he turned, and spoke in low, deep tones.

"Let the people enter." he said.

Forthwith the six priests rose from their kneeling posture, and passing out of the alcove, made their way to the main entrance of the temple.

In the meantime, Wu Ling passed across to the foot of the Buddha, and waited there for the people to come in. They came at the summons of the priests—one by one with bowed heads. The temple was scarcely large enough to hold them, but there was no pushing—no unseemly hurry.

Each one took his place, and when all were there, Wu Ling held up his hand.

"My people," he said solemnly, "You are gathered here to-night for the great ceremony. I have let it be known that tonight, when the moon reaches its zenith, there shall be made to the god Mo"—here Wu Ling bent his head, while the rest followed his example—"a sacrifice such as delights the heart of the blessed one. Here in the island of Kaitu we have reared to the God a temple, which in truth is poor enough, but which is the best our feeble efforts can fashion. To him the glory of the heavens we bow in submission this night, and to him we make sacrifice.

"Before casting upon the altar the food which the god craves, I shall tell you why the sacrifice will be particularly welcome to him. Listen, my people! I have but come from a far country—a stronghold of the hated whites. While there I saw many things, and did many things. Also I formed a temporary alliance with one of the whites, in which I was to help him in certain things for his aid out here. I kept my word to him, but even at the moment of victory was the prize snatched from me.

"And, my people, whom think you was the cause? Remember you the days of old, when on the ground in front of this very temple I was cast down, and the hands of the white dog went to my throat. Remember you the man who, as you all thought, sent me to the arms of the blessed Confucius?

"It was he, and he it was who fell into my hands. But again he escaped, and that even while I was near to Kaitu. He it was whom I intended to be the sacrifice to the blessed god Mo. But he escaped. Yet there fell into my hands one who will also please the god. I speak of the one who will form the sacrifice this night.

"He is the heart of the man whom I lost. He is with him at all times. He is to him what the faithful San is to me. It is the lad whom the man Blake always has with him. Ah! Indeed will the god Mo be pleased this night. And on that altar will this white one feed the flames. Now you will see him prepared for that altar."

Wu Ling's voice died away, and he stood motionless while two of the priests slipped away to the room at the rear of the temple. They returned a few minutes later, leading between them a figure garbed in white—a figure whose hands were bound, but whose head was proudly erect.

The two priests conducted him along to the feet of the Buddha, and stood him so he could be seen by the whole assembly.

It was Tinker—Tinker, white as a sheet, with the strain and his whiteness enhanced by the white garments in which he had been clad, but a Tinker whose head was held proudly, and whose eyes never faltered as they gazed out at the hostile crowd before him.

At the sight of him a low murmur rose from the assembly, and this soon resolved itself into a sort of chant which Wu Ling took up and beat time to. It was the chant to the god Mo.

When it was finished, Wu Ling raised his hand and again spoke.

"There is more to tell you, my people," he said. "Into my hands there fell another—a woman. She it is who is the apple of the man Blake's eye. She it is who loves the man Blake, though she strives hard to hide it. But think you the secrets of the stupid white pigs are hid from the gaze of the East? They are transparent as the water in yonder lagoon.

"She goes not to the sacrificial altar, since it is forbidden to make sacrifice of that sex. But she goes to grace my house, and thus for ever will be hidden from the gaze of man. No vengeance against the man Blake could be greater than that. You shall see her my people."

Again Wu Lings's voice died away, and two more of the priests disappeared towards the room at the rear. A minute or more passed, during which all eyes were turned expectantly in the direction of the rear room, then slowly the great stone door swung wide, and the two priests entered, leading between another white-clad figure.

It was Yvonne.

Fancy, if you can, the scene. A barbaric Eastern temple, redolent of mystery and incense—a hot tropic night, with the land breeze just floating down from the jungle-clad hinterland—the sickly odour of the mangroves from the swamp by the lagoon—the sweet smell of the paw-paw blossoms, and the soft rustling of the palms—over all the great bowl of night, with its thousands of stars riding supremely beautiful, and reflected in the limpid waters of the lagoon.

Then the wild, savage-looking crew which was gathered in the temple—yellow and seamed Chinese, brown and nearly naked Malays, Alfours, Cingalese, not a few Japs who had given up their own country. Javanese, Sumatrese, Kanakas, Polynesians from the outer islands. Dayaks from Borneo, and the Celebes and Melanesians from as far south as New Guinea and the Solomons.

There they stood, wildly clad and wild-souled, held under the spell of the man they looked upon as a demi-god, and swayed utterly by his every word—standing in hungry regard of the two whites whom the Illustrious One had brought home with him—the one to go as a living sacrifice to the god Mo—the other to share as awful a fate.

As for Tinker, who stood with head held high, only he himself knew what he was suffering, and had suffered. From the moment when he and Yvonne had been dragged out of the boats and taken aboard the tramp, it had not been hard for him to guess that Wu Ling would have little mercy on him.

But though he realised the danger of his own position, Tinker was glad that at least Blake was free. Yet his heart bled for Yvonne. He understood enough of the rough dialect which Wu Ling had used in speaking to his motley crew to gather what the prince's intentions were regarding Yvonne. She would go to be his wife—to be the wife of a Celestial.

When he thought of Yvonne, in her winsome loveliness, being forced to become the wife of a Celestial, prince though he might be, all the control which he had guarded so well threatened to break its bounds and send him dashing in among the crew about him in a mad and a futile endeavour to wreak vengeance upon them.

Mad and futile it would have been, for what could one lad, however valiant he might be, do against that mob?

As Yvonne was led forward, Tinker's eyes met hers. What did those two so very much alone there say to each other in those glances? It was a mutual message of courage and trust.

Yvonne, garbed in a long, white gown which had been provided for her, stood proudly erect, with her glorious bronze-gold hair rippling over her shoulders like a stream of molten copper. Her skin looked even whiter than usual, and her throat gleamed like a beautiful pillar of pure alabaster. Her feet were clad in sandals—her hands hung loosely by her side. She looked like the incarnation of some goddess of old.

As the eyes of the savage assembly looked upon the white captive who would go to grace the house of their chief, a low murmur of admiration broke out. It was forgotten in that moment that she was of the hated whites. Her beauty conquered them as it had conquered others. But even her beauty would not save her from the fate which was to be hers.

Yet her eyes, heavy with fatigue, and large and shadowy from the effects of the strain under which she had been, again looked into Tinker's.

"Don't give up," she whispered, so he could hear. "He is doing all he can, you may be sure"—"he" meaning Blake, as both knew.

Tinker smiled bravely. "I am not afraid," he replied. "I am worrying for you."

The next moment a heavy hand was swept across his mouth, cutting off all further speech.

Then, Wu Ling spoke again.

"My people," he said, "behold the woman. Behold the one who goes to the house of your chief. Behold the illustrious pearl which I plucked from the lap of the whites. It is indeed fitting that the one of all who is precious to the man Blake should become the property of Prince Wu Ling.

"Now, before she is to be taken away, never more to see the world from the outside, she will witness the sacrifice to the blessed god Mo. Let the altar be prepared."

With that, the low chant to the god Mo broke out again, and as it rose and swelled on the tropic night Wu Ling turned towards the alcove wherein squatted the golden god, now looking grim and hideous under the slanting rays of the moon, which came in through an opening at the rear of the alcove.

When those rays struck the god full on the top of the head, the moon would be at the zenith. Then would the sacrifice be made according to the ancient rites.

Two priests shuffled across to the great porphyry altar, where burned the fire of sacrifice. Two more dragged Tinker along to the altar while the other two forced Yvonne to walk nearer to it.

The whole assembly strained forward, still chanting the barbaric wail, and waiting eagerly for what was to come.

Tinker was held upright before the altar, then, with a single sweep of the hand, his white garment was torn from him revealing him clad only in a white loincloth. Beneath the ruddy reflection of the altar flames, he looked like a young Adonis, standing white and slim and erect, his limbs clean cut and straight, his head and features like an old cameo.

Verily the god Mo was out to receive a worthy sacrifice, which would appease even his Molochian appetite.

Wu Ling approached the altar, and, bending his head before the god, chanted a prayer which was echoed by the assembly behind him. Then the prince stood aside, and the two priests who held Tinker dragged him slowly forward towards the altar on which the fire burned.

Yvonne stood like a statue, her hands pressed against her breast, her eyes full of a nameless terror, and her limbs frozen with horror.

As the lad was dragged nearer and nearer, her breast rose and fell in an increasing agony of suffocation, until finally her suffering broke all bounds, and her lips opened.

Then, on the tropic night, there rang out a passionate cry for succour—a cry which was caught by the vaulted roof of the temple, and echoed and re-echoed throughout the place, to go wailing with rising cadence through the palms which stretched to the lagoon.

In her desperation she had called upon the man she loved—she had called upon Sexton Blake.

When he was quite convinced that Beauremon was telling the truth and that his visit to the T.B.D, was no scheme to catch them in ambush, Blake lost no time in preparing for the rescue party to go ashore.

He knew that if Wu Ling said he would carry out certain intentions regarding Tinker and Yvonne he would do so, unless some power stronger than himself prevented him.

Whatever way he looked at it, one had to acknowledge that Yvonne and Tinker were in an extremely hazardous position. In the hands of a savage crew, whose law was the word of their chief, they stood little show of leniency. And if what Beauremon said was true, then when the moon reached its zenith, rescue of any kind would be out of the question.

In a few minutes Blake lived years. His mind leaped back to the years which Tinker had been with him. He recollected the first early days of their friendship when the young street urchin had been of great value to him.

Then he recalled the time which had followed when the lad had developed from the urchin into a fine specimen of youth, and how by diligent study and application he had made of himself not only a charming, but a cultured young fellow such as one rarely met with.

Then came the memory of the dangers through which they had passed together—of struggles and triumphs, of sicknesses and recoveries, of joys and sorrows which they had shared together.

And, thinking, a lump rose in his throat, and the limpid waters of the lagoon became suddenly obscured by the mist which filled his eyes. Was the end of it all to be such as this night seemed to promise? Was the lad, so fine and stalwart and clean, to go to form the living sacrifice to a barbaric golden god?

Not while Sexton Blake lived and breathed and was able to fight. And if he were too late then he would wreak such a vengeance upon the despoilers of the lad as the deepest mind in China could not conceive.

Then his thoughts went to Yvonne—Yvonne whom he had first met when she was a wayward, whimsical girl—Yvonne who had been to him what no other woman had been. He remembered how with her wilfulness she had at times made him sad, and then how, with her sweet surrender, she would relent and try to make up for it all.

There were times—ah! he scarcely dared think of them. And one thing stood out clear and distinct as a star shining to a man in the void. That was the warm pressure of her lips on his when he lay weak and exhausted in the bunk on board the Fleur-de-Lys. His pulse throbbed at the memory, and the cords in his wrists stood out as he thought of the yellow hands of Wu Ling laid upon her.

With that thought his anger broke bounds. With a savage exclamation he turned to the commander of the T.B.D.

"Commander Porter," he said, "will you authorise a landing-party to rescue the two British subjects who have fallen into the clutches of these Celestials?"

The commander looked back at Blake with sympathy in his eyes. He had seen something of what the stern-looking Englishman was suffering.

He nodded briefly.

"The resources of the ship are at your disposal, Mr. Blake. I shall give orders at once to have a landing-party got ready and then we shall go ashore. Before we have finished with these people we shall teach them a lesson they will remember for many a long day. I shall also send a party aboard that tramp to take possession of her.

"Fortunately I sent a wireless to the commander-in-chief of this station asking his permission to act as I thought best in this emergency, and he has instructed me to do so."

Blake nodded his thanks, and then the low voices of the officers rang out as they went to muster the landing-party.

Blake turned to Beauremon.

"Will you come?" he asked curtly.

The baron shrugged.

"I have no particular score to settle with Wu Ling," he said, with all his old sang froid. "But still it was a bit crude of him to order me to be cut up in the jungle to-day, so, with your permission, I think I will join you, Mr. Blake."

As the boats were lowered and brought round, the crews tumbled in, and while one of them rowed across to take possession of the tramp, two more made for the shore.

Blake, who had been at Kaitu in the past, took the lead when they had tumbled out on to the beach, and with drawn cutlasses, they started through the trees.

On they went, foot by foot, with the utmost caution and striving to anticipate any possible ambush.

Half-way through the grove of palms and paw-paw trees Blake paused and held up a warning hand. They heard a low murmur which rose and fell and rose again as a chant—and chant it was to the savage god Mo, as Blake well knew.

Then it stopped, and they were about to go ahead again when loud and clear in the ringing urgency there came a cry for succour—a cry full of terror and laden with horror—a cry in a voice which sent Blake's pulses hammering madly.

It was Yvonne's voice.

That was the last thing needed to make Blake fling all caution to the winds.

With an exclamation he turned to those behind him.

"Follow!" he cried. "Follow to the temple!"

Drawing his revolver, he dashed on through the grove with the others tearing after him. Into the opening where stood the village they burst, and racing down between the palm-thatched huts which rested on piles they made for the temple which Blake knew stood at the other end of the village.

Again he heard Yvonne's voice raised in a cry of frantic appeal, then it was cut off suddenly. Blake was several strides in advance, with Commander Porter and Beauremon next, and the panting crew of the T.B.D. tumbling along after with their cutlasses drawn and their eyes alight with the joy of battle.

Whatever may have been Beauremon's attitude in the past when he was for the nonce an ally. There were old scores to settle between him and Blake which no attitude of the present could wipe out. But the call of the white had clutched him, and in the final test he had, as many more, answered the call.

Blake had always had a certain respect for the baron, for he had always fought according to the creed of the gentleman until his recent alliance with Wu Ling. There had been a little affair in South America not long before when Beauremon and Rymer had tried to steal a republic, and in which, by keen strategy, Blake had outwitted the pair.

In that affair, as in others, Beauremon had remained cool and nonchalant, while undoubtedly Rymer had sadly lost his temper. And a man who could command the sang froid which was Beauremon's, always roused Blake's admiration.

Nor could he ever forget that it was Beauremon who had swum out to warn him of what was afoot in Kaitu that night.

As the party dashed towards the temple, a wandering pig crossed from beneath one of the huts, and seeing the advancing horde racing towards it had raced off with a startled squeal. An old woman, too old to attend the assembly at the temple, saw them go by and gave vent to a shrill scream.

But they were beyond caution now, and when the temple finally came in sight they raised a mighty cheer as they raced for the steps.

Up them dashed Blake, followed by Beauremon and Commander Porter, and in to the sacred precincts of the temple went Blake, his automatic held ready for action.

As they broke through the main entrance into the crowd of savages which was gathered there, a strange sight met their eyes. Over the heads of the assembly they could see Wu Ling in his yellow robes of priesthood standing by the altar on which burned a fierce fire.

Beside him, and in the very act of lifting a bound figure upon the altar, were two priests clad in yellow and white. Near at hand was a figure in white—a woman clutching her heaving breast and gazing with eyes of horror at the altar to which the slim figure of the lad was being dragged.

Behind the altar two other priests were standing ready to attend to the sacrifice when it should be laid upon the block of porphyry. And over all sounded the barbaric sacrificial chant of the assembly.

It was a weird scene. And into that scene tore Sexton Blake, followed by Commander Porter and a crew of British bluejackets eager for a fight.

How to describe the pandemonium which followed. The chant of those nearest the door changed into a startled squeal as the party entered, and there were wild reaching for cutlasses and knives.

Blake, who had eyes for only one thing, the lad who was being hoisted to the altar, levelled his revolver and pulled the trigger twice in rapid succession.

First one then the other of the two priests who were lifting the lad to the altar threw up their hands and fell forward, one of them striking the altar fairly and dropping into the flames—an unwilling sacrifice to the god he professed to worship.

The other went tumbling to the floor at the foot of the altar, while the lad in the white loincloth stumbled to his knees, safe but still bound.

With a loud cheer the bluejackets now took a hand, and as they dashed into the thick of the yellow crew Blake fought and shot his way through to the front of the temple where Yvonne was held by two priests.

They, in panic and at the command of Wu Ling, started to drag her towards the room at the rear of the temple, but Blake shot over the heads of the crowd and sent her captors reeling back.

He next turned his weapon on Wu Ling, who he saw making for the spot where squatted the god Mo, but at that moment a struggling party of Celestial and bluejackets crashed into him and his bullet went wild.

The next moment Wu Ling disappeared. The very floor seemed to have swallowed him up.

Blake kept on until he came to Yvonne, who had stumbled to her knees. Catching her in his arms he lifted her up and held her tight, and as her white face became upturned to to his, Blake saw that the strain had been too much for her—she had fainted—which was well.

Laying her down in a safe place he loosened her bonds and made for Tinker.

"I'm all right, guv'nor," whispered the lad weakly, as Blake picked him up like a baby and carried him across to where he had left Yvonne. "Bit of a strain, but you came in time."

"You plucky lad," muttered Blake with choking utterance. "If they had done that thing to you I should have followed Wu Ling to the ends of the earth. But, thank Heaven, I was in time. One moment, my lad, and I will have you free."

All this time the fight in the main part of the temple was raging fiercely. Commander Porter, Lieutenant Trepwitt—Midshipman Fortescue had been sent to take charge of the party which had boarded the tramp—and Beauremon were leading the bluejackets and were fighting with a will.

Caught like rats in a trap, there was nothing for the Celestials to do but to fight. There was no way of escape but by the main entrance to the temple, and between them and that entrance were the British bluejackets, just getting warmed up to their work.

It was, in the words of one of them, a glorious scrap. Back and forth the fighting, cursing crowd swayed, cutlasses rising and falling, knives flashing and men going down in all directions.

Methodically the bluejackets were driving their men towards the altar, and if they succeeded in getting them there they would literally cut them to pieces.

Blake, who had been busy with the two who meant so much to him, watched the progress of the fight, even as he strove to revive Yvonne, and as the crowd came nearer and nearer to him he lifted her up again to carry her to a place of greater safety.

Then, as he held her to his breast, her eyes opened and the fear in them died out as she saw whom it was who held her.

"Oh, it is you!" she breathed.

Blake looked down at her. She seemed very small and very sweet, and very helpless in that moment, and as he bent his head her lips came perilously close to his.

A strand of her soft hair floated across his face and the sweet perfume of it filled him. Then his head went lower, his eyes gazed deeply into hers, her lips parted ever so little, and with a red mist suffusing his eyes Blake pressed her to him, kissing her warm lips fiercely.

The next moment, shaken and trembling from head to foot with a strange, exquisite feeling, he forced his way through to the open air. Tinker followed, and as they got outside they could tell by the sounds within that the bluejackets were forcing the enemy back to the altar.

Just as victory was within their grasp there sounded a sudden rumbling, and the walls of the temple split asunder. They fell to the ground with a roar, and as the stone and dust flew in all directions, bluejackets and Celestials staggered into the open air, coughing and spluttering.

In a moment Blake had grasped what had happened. Wu Ling, who had so strangely disappeared, had not been unprepared for some such contingency as this. Blake's previous visit to the island had taught the prince something.

When he disappeared by the god Mo, he had left the temple by a secret passage and had touched a switch which had blown the walls asunder.

How that struggling horde managed to reach the open air without more casualties was a mystery, but on both sides there were few left within the ruins. Then with the true spirit of the fight which had gripped them, they renewed the struggle. But here the bluejackets redoubled their efforts, and after a sharp struggle the Celestials broke and fled for the safety of the jungle.

The bluejackets went in pursuit, but once the Celestials spread out in the almost impenetrable jungle, it was useless to persist. So Commander Porter whistled for his dogs of war to return, and they gathered by the temple to take toll of the casualties.

They were far less than they had thought would be the case. Two men had gone down in the fight in the temple, while two more had been caught beneath the falling walls. Four deaths in all, with a good many minor wounds.

Of the Celestials they found nine dead and half a dozen cases with severe wounds. So far the honours were with the landing-party.

Now the island of Kaitu is not large as islands go. It rises abruptly from the yellow waters of the China Sea, being the submerged fragment of part of that once great stretch of continent which, in ages past, linked up the Dutch East Indies with Papua and Australia.

It is not an atoll, as one sees in the Polynesian Islands of the South Pacific, but a mountain-top of the old continental shelf, and, like all those peaks which now form the Solomons, New Guinea, and the Dutch East Indies, it possesses a high, jungle-clad, and almost impenetrable hinterland.

Only too well did Sexton Blake know how difficult it would be to follow Wu Ling and his men into those dank, humid depths. Once in the past had he and Tinker attempted to force their way into the country where the hill men held sway, and he still retained the memory of that disastrous affair.

Yet the chase for Wu Ling had been a long one. Was he to leave Kaitu, knowing that Wu Ling was still on the island and unharmed? Every inclination of Blake's nature rebelled against such an idea.

Yvonne and Tinker had been in the grip of the Yellow Tiger, and had the torpedo-boat destroyer arrived only a little later, their fate would have been a terrible one. By now Tinker would have gone into the brazen maw of the god Mo. And Yvonne—ah, Heaven only knew what her fate would have been!

Gazing at the white, drawn face of the girl, whose lips had clung to his such a short time before, Blake vowed that he would go after Wu Ling, and stay on his trail until he had captured him, or killed him.

Once and for all he would wipe from the face of the earth the man who was such a menace to society at large. Wu Ling must be scotched.

With this determination in his mind Blake approached Commander Porter, and, drawing him aside, said:

"I have been thinking over things. I know this island pretty well, and I know exactly how difficult it will be to follow the fugitives into the bush. They may go in as deeply as possible, or they may lurk near the lagoon—we can't tell. But I am much mistaken in my estimate of Wu Ling, if he has not prepared a retreat in the jungle.

"We razed this place once before, and the very perfection of his arrangements here leads me to think that he was not unprepared for any contingency. At the same time I am strongly in favour of hunting him out and ending his career, once and for all. What do you think?"

Commander Porter stroked his beard thoughtfully.

"I am quite prepared to base all calculations on your statements, Blake. You have already proved that you know the island and the man. If you think it advisable to follow them up and make a final settlement with them, I am ready to give you the men with which to do so, but you can understand that I don't want to lose any of my men unnecessarily."

"I realise that, Commander Porter. I will be quite frank with you. The jungle is thick, and if Wu Ling had made some sort of treaty with the hill men who live in the hinterland, then the advance into the jungle will be fraught with extreme danger.

"We are bound to have some casualties—they may be light, or, on the other hand, if the hill men make a strong effort to oppose our advance, then they may be heavy. All the same, I am inclined to think that the object is worth the risk."

"I'll tell you what I will do, Blake," responded the commander, after a moment or two. "I will call my men together, and put the proposal to them. All those who volunteer may go, and I myself will accompany you as well."

Commander Porter spoke to one of his men who stood near, instructing him to call together in front of the ruins of the temple, and, taking up his stand in front of them, the commander addressed them:

"My men," he said, "you have done splendidly to-day. We have achieved part of our purpose on coming here, and before we leave we shall raze this place to the ground. But the man whom we hoped to capture has escaped into the jungle. This man—the arch-mind who rules the Celestial Brotherhood, which is such a menace to the white races of the earth—still goes free.

"Mr. Sexton Blake, who stands beside me, knows the island as well as any white man living. He does not underestimate the dangers and difficulties of penetrating into the jungle in pursuit of the man we want, but he thinks it can be done, and, if possible to get sufficient volunteers to go, he will undertake it. I may say that I shall accompany him.

"Do any of you wish to volunteer for the attempt? Bear in mind I do not ask you to go. If you do so, it will only be your own free will. All those who wish to do so will take one step forward."

The commander broke off then and waited. There was a restless sort of rustling along the ranks of the men, then, as one big bluejacket at the end of the front rank stepped forward, every bluejacket on the semi-circle followed his suit.

The commander smiled as he saw the result of his words.

"I thought I knew my men," he said with satisfaction, as he turned back to Blake.

Blake nodded.

"They didn't need to be asked," he replied. "Men who fight as they fought to-day are not the men to hang back for all the hill men in the China Sea. I think, Commander Porter, that the sooner we start the better."

Scarcely had Blake uttered the words, when a man suddenly burst through from the cover of the grove between the village and the lagoon. As he ran up they saw it was one of the bluejackets, who had gone aboard the tramp with Midshipman Fortescue. He paused when he reached Commander Porter, and, saluting, said:

"Mr. Fortescue's compliments, sir, and he begs to inform you that the yacht, Fleur-de-Lys, has just come into the lagoon. He wishes to know, sir, if he may permit Mr. Graves to land?"

Commander Porter nodded his head.

"My compliments to Mr. Fortescue, and tell him to permit Mr. Graves to come ashore."

Saluting, the bluejacket turned, and made off. A little later they saw Graves coming through the trees.

It was a strange reunion which he and Yvonne had there before the ruins of the temple, but in that moment they showed how truly deep was the affection which existed between them.

When it had been arranged that Yvonne should go on board the yacht at once, Blake prepared to start for the jungle. He himself took the lead, with Tinker directly behind him, followed by Commander Porter.

Then came the long file of bluejackets, with Lieutenant Trepwitt bringing up the rear.

Slowly, and with infinite caution Blake advanced. He knew he could not get far until morning came, but he was determined to accomplish as much as possible in order to anticipate any counter-move which Wu Ling might attempt.

He knew, too, that during the first part of the journey they would meet with less danger than when they go further along. It would be when they were climbing the trail to the hinterland that they would need every ounce of caution.

The hill men of those islands have some nice little traps for the unwary, one pleasant diversion is to bend down a sapling in the thickest part of the jungle, and to fasten it so that one passing along the faint track, which is known as the trail, must strike it.

The veriest touch releases a poisoned spear, which has been carefully arranged at the height of a man's heart, and before he can save himself he is lying on the ground in the throes of violent convulsions.

Again they find particular pleasure in concealing beneath the thick mulch which has gathered on the trail a small poisoned bar, which the unwary may walk upon. Result—sudden death.

To add to these diversions the hill men have a faculty of loitering along close to the trail screened by the almost impenetrable jungle on either side, and from the safety of this retreat to wing forth poisoned arrows against the unwary. In fact, they are quite a pleasant people those hill men.

Sexton Blake had had more than one sample of their pleasantry in the past, and for this reason he exercised a caution which struck the bluejackets as somewhat unnecessary.

But before that small band got out of the jungle again they thanked their stars that it had been Sexton Blake who had led them into the jungle-clad hinterland.

The roseate hues of dawn were just suffusing the sky when Blake halted at the end of the swampy lowland, at the spot where the upward climb to the hinterland began.

There he reapportioned the loads of arms and ammunition, saw that his party was all right, sent back two men who showed signs of fever, and, lining them up, once more began the climb.

As the hours passed a dim twilight spread through the forest, but never for a single moment did they get a glimpse of the sun. In the heart of those great jungle aisles, twilight, and the dank humidity of the tropics, held perpetual sway.

It was ten o'clock by Blake's watch before they came upon anything which seemed to indicate that their progress would be disputed.

It was one of those spear traps which, cautiously though he was advancing, Blake sprang. As the sapling flew upwards the poisoned spear shot forth from the screen of thick leaves, behind which it had been hidden, flying with a vicious swish past Blake's shoulder, butted itself in a great bank of ferns on the other side of the trail.

Blake paused for a moment, then, watching carefully for a second trap, started on again.

Another hour went by, and though the air was still intensely heavy, there was still a fresher feeling in it than there had been farther back, proving that they were steadily climbing higher.

It was broad noon when, as he suddenly came out upon a wide opening in the forest, the first definite attack came. Then it burst upon them with fierce suddeness.

From the cover of the trees opposite them, a perfect hail of poisoned spears and arrows came flying across the tiny glade.

Blake sprang back quickly, and sharply ordered his men to take cover. Like clumsy elephants, the seamen plunged into the thick screen on either side of the trail, with Blake, Tinker and Commander Porter following closely.

But even then one of the poisoned arrows struck a bluejacket in the breast, and even as he plunged for cover dropped in convulsions of death.

Blake rapped out his orders sharp and clear.

"Make ready to fire!" he ordered. "Ready—fire!"

He himself had snatched up a rifle, and, aiming it at the trees on the other side of the open space, began to fire as rapidly as possible.

A fusillade broke out on all sides, as the bluejackets followed suit, and from the cover of the trees across the glade there came the sound of shrill screams, as the bullets found a mark.

The shower of spears and arrows suddenly stopped, and when Blake gave the order to stop firing, there regained a silence strangely at variance with the pandemonium which only a few moments before had filled the surrounding jungle.

Springing out into the open, Blake called upon his men to follow.

"They will have taken to the jungle," he said rapidly to Commander Porter, who had joined him. "We shall have to be on our watch for the next move."

Going forward, Blake made boldly for the trees across the glade, and plunging into the forest again, started along a trail which was far more distinct than that by which they had travelled during the morning.

A few hundred yards or so he went, before he received the second surprise. Once more he saw that the forest opened up, and as he came out into the open he saw a sight that held him breathless with wonder.

Before him was a sheer descent of open country, which dropped away for a half mile or more. Here and there rose giant trees, which gave it almost the appearance of an English park.

At the foot of the first drop there lay a wide lake, limpid and black in its mysterious beauty.

Suddenly there flashed upon Blake a strange rumour he had heard from the salt-water men of the lagoon. They had told him, in times gone past, of a sacred lake in the interior of the island.

Until then Blake had thought the whole story but a myth. But now he knew that he had come upon the very lake which had been spoken of, and in some way he knew that it was connected with the worship of the golden god Mo.

In a flash he knew that it was here Wu Ling had fled from the temple, and it would be here that they must meet again.

He approached the edge of the drop, and standing easily, gazed down at the expanse of park-like country which stretched before him.

Commander Porter and the bluejackets followed him, and stood about him, waiting for the next word.

Even as they waited, there came to them across the black waters of the lake of a great voice, which droned, sweeping up in deep cadences to the brink on which stood the small body of white men.

"Go back! Go back!" said the voice. "You who desecrate this sacred spot of the god Mo will suffer as man never suffered!"

Then the voice died away, and Blake shaking himself free from the uncanny feeling which threatened to sweep over him, and which he could see had already gripped some of the bluejackets, drew his revolver and dashed down the incline.

"Come on, men!" he cried. "Let us clean out this hole!"

The calm confidence of his voice jerked them out of the spell which was sweeping over them, and, with a loud cheer, the bluejackets tore down the incline after him.

At the same moment a horde of Malays and Celestials appeared close to the edge of the lake, and, screaming with rage, charged up the hill.

They were armed with knives, cutlasses, and rifles, but now that they actually saw that which menaced them, the bluejackets steadied down wonderfully, spreading out to take cover whenever possible, started firing as the went.

Still the savages came on, though many of them went down beneath the hail of lead which the bluejackets poured into them.

Then, when scarcely a hundred yards separated the two forces, Blake gave the order to charge.

With a loud yell the bluejackets sprang from cover and raced forward. They crashed into the front rank of the enemy a few moments later, and in the park which sloped to the edge of that sacred lake there ensued a fight which for savagery and fierceness could scarcely be excelled.

Through the press of the struggle Blake caught a fleeting glimpse of Wu Ling urging on his men to destroy the white men. But, back at the temple, the bluejackets had got the measure of the foe, and now, fighting with cool confidence, they steadily drove them back.

Foot by foot, yard by yard, they retreated, until they stood at the very edge of the black waters of the lake. There the Celestials and Malays made another desperate stand; but Commander Porter cried to his men to strike and strike hard, and, led by Blake and the commander, the whites dashed forward with renewed vigour.

Under the intense onslaught the yellow men wavered, broke, tried to recover, broke again, and dashing down their weapons fled.

Springing out of the crush of the fight, Blake singled out Wu Ling, and keeping his eyes on the yellow tunic of the flying prince, tore along the bank of the lake in pursuit.

A hundred yards or more the prince fled, until ahead there appeared a wide shelf of stone.

There he drew up, and standing at the very edge of the shelf, turned back and faced Blake.

Blake saw Wu Ling raise both hands over his head, saw his eyes flash eternal hatred, saw in them the promise of vengeance, then the prince dived down into the black waters of the lake, which ripped under the impact of his body and closed over his head.

Blake stopped, panting, at the edge of the shelf of stone, and leaning over, gazed down at the lake, waiting for the head of Wu Ling to reappear.

Before he would let the prince escape he, too, would dive into the lake and finish the fight there.

A minute passed, and still Wu Ling did not come to the surface. Two minutes went by, and the black waters of the lake remained limpid as ever.

Three, four, five minutes crawled passed, and then Blake straightened up.

"Suicide," he muttered. "Still, I can scarcely believe that Wu Ling would give in so easily. However, that settles it, and there is nothing to do but to get back to the lagoon as quickly as possible. If the hill men make a fresh attack, things may turn out badly for us."

So it was that a little over an hour later the small party of white men started back along the trail for the coast. It was full evening when they finally came out again to the village, for their return had been retarded owing to the wounded, whom they had been compelled to carry.

In front of the temple, the exhausted party drew to answer the roll call. Then, in charge of Lieutenant Trepwitt, the bluejackets prepared to return to the T.B.D.

When the wounded had been attended to, a party was told to look after the dead.

Sexton Blake stayed behind in order to make a thorough search of the temple. In what had been the alcove devoted to the god Mo he found the golden figure of the god lying on its face, its jade base still intact and beautiful. Blake had it hoisted up and carried down to the beach, the one trophy he wished to take away with him. Then with a party of men he started in and razed the village to the ground, burning it from end to end.

In the blanket of the smoke they retreated to the lagoon and went aboard the yacht, leaving the island to its ruins, its jungle, and what that jungle hid.

As red morn flaunted upwards in the east, the blunt nose of the T.B.D. led the way out to set through the mangrove-lined passage, followed by the slim and rakish-looking Fleur-de-Lys with the tramp bringing up the rear. Dipping a curtsey to the soft caress of the China Sea they sailed away, leaving Wu Ling to brood in his jungle.

Beauremon came with them as far as Batavia, and there they left him. The T.B.D. had gone off with her prize to report, and with its own happy party on board the Fleur-de-Lys sailed through the tropic seas for England.

So ended the strange chase which grew out of the kidnapping of the Munitions Minister by the Yellow Tiger.

*   *   *   *   *

Nor did Sexton Blake dream that as they slipped out to sea from the purple lagoon, which had been their anchorage, a tall Celestial stood on the stone shelf, back at the edge of the sacred lake, with his hands stretched high to Heaven, cursing the whites who had desecrated the retreat of the god Mo, and vowing vengeance on the one man who had led them to that retreat. The waters of the sacred lake had closed over the head of Wu Ling, but in their limpid depths he had not found his grave. Beneath that stone shelf was a cunningly constructed tunnel leading to an underground chamber, where Wu Ling, as High Priest on Earth of the god Mo made worship of his deity. Well was the sacred lake called in Chinese the Lake of

Concealment.

THE END.

[63500 WORDS]